Oscar Wilde

THE PICTURE OF DORIAN GRAY

Illustrated by Tanja Aldebot

EASY READERS · ER · EASY READERS

The vocabulary is based on
Michael West: A General Service List of
English Words, revised & enlarged edition, 1953
Birger Thorйn: 10.000 Words for 10 Years of English, 1990
J.A. van Ek: The Threshold Level,
Council of Europe Press, 1990
The British National Corpus, Oxford, 1996

Series editor: Ulla Malmmose

Cover illustration: Tanja Aldebot

ISBN Denmark 978-87-23-90722-6
www.easyreaders.eu

The CEFR levels stated on the back of the book
are approximate levels.

Easy Readers EGMONT

Printed in Denmark by
Sangill Grafisk Produktion, Holme-Olstrup

OSCAR WILDE (1854–1900)
was born and educated in Dublin, Ireland before he moved to England to study at Oxford University, where he won a poetry prize. After giving lecture tours in the USA and Canada, he returned to London and married Constance Mary Lloyd (1858–1898) with whom he had two sons: Cyril (1885–1915), who was killed during World War I, and Vyvyan (1886–1976), who was the author of a memoir *Son of Oscar Wilde* (1954) and *Oscar Wilde: A Pictorial Biography* in 1960.

The Wildes settled in Chelsea, London where Oscar continued to write and work for such magazines as the *Pall Mall Gazette* and became editor of *Woman's World* in 1887. In the same year he wrote a famous story about a funny ghost, *The Canterville Ghost* (1887, see the old b/w film!) followed by some famous children's stories, *The Happy Prince and Other Tales* (1888) and *The Picture of Dorian Gray* (1891). However, Wilde was best-known as a playwright, and *Lady Windermere's Fan* (1892), *A Woman of No Importance* (1893), *An Ideal Husband* (1895), and *The Importance of Being Earnest* (1895) are still performed today. The last-mentioned story of 'Bunbury' is a classic that has been translated into many languages.

In 1891 Wilde, who as a young man had had homosexual experiences, met the much younger English poet Lord Alfred Douglas, nicknamed 'Bosie' (1870–1945) and fell in love with him. Their gay affair shocked the country, as well as Mrs Wilde, who divorced him, took the boys away and changed her name. Bosie's father helped to get Oscar Wilde arrested and he was convicted of 'gross indecency' for homosexual acts, despite his defence of 'the love that dare not speak its name'. He was sentenced to two years hard labour, most of which he served in Reading Gaol, where he was inspired to write the brilliant poem, *Ballad of Reading Gaol*, against the death penalty and hanging of Charles Wooldridge

After his release from prison, Wilde was a broken man in ill-health. He adopted the name Sebastian Melmoth and went to Paris, where he was reunited with another lover, the Canadian journalist Robert 'Robbie' Ross (1869–1918). On his deathbed, Wilde was baptised into the Roman Catholic Church and received Extreme Unction. He died of meningitis on 30 November 1900 and is buried in Père Lachaise cemetery in Paris.

A fascinating film of Oscar Wilde was made in 1997, *Wilde*, starring Stephen Fry.

Persons in the book

Dorian Gray — a beautiful young man
Basil Hallward — an artist who is painting Dorian Gray
Lord Henry Wotton ('Harry') — a friend of Dorian
Sybil Vane — an actress
Mrs Vane — her mother
James Vane — her brother

Contents

Chapter 1

The studio was filled with the smell of the *lilac* that came through the open door. From the corner of the divan covered with a Persian carpet Lord Henry Wotton could see the branches of cherry trees in blossom that made him think of Japanese paintings. The distant roar of London came here as the sound of a far-away organ. In the centre of the room on an *easel* stood a full-length portrait of a young man of extraordinary beauty. In front of it, a little distance away, sat the artist himself, Basil Hallward.

As the painter looked at the gracious and lovely youth he had so skilfully mirrored in his art, a smile of pleasure passed across his face. But he suddenly closed his eyes and placed his fingers upon the lids as though he wanted to keep in his brain some curious dream from which he feared to awake.

"It is your best work, Basil, the best thing you have ever done," said Lord Henry. "You must certainly send it next year to the *Grosvenor*. The *Academy* is too large and too vulgar. Whenever I went there, there were either so many people

---

lilac, tree with pink or white, sweet-smelling flowers
easel, wooden frame to hold a picture during painting
Grosvenor, London hotel
Academy, The Royal Art Academy

that I was not able to see the pictures, which was bad, or so many pictures that I was not able to see the people, which was worse. The Grosvenor is really the only place."

"I don't think I shall send it anywhere," answered Basil.

Lord Henry raised his eyebrows and looked at him in amazement.

"Not send it anywhere? What odd chaps you painters are! You will do anything in the world to gain a *reputation*, and as soon as you get one, you seem to want to throw it away. That is silly, for there is only one thing in the world worse than being talked about and that is not being talked about. A portrait like this would put you far above all the young men in England."

"I know you will laugh at me," Basil replied, "but I really can't *exhibit* it. I have put too much of myself into it."

Lord Henry stretched himself out on the divan and laughed: "Too much of yourself in it! I really can't see any *resemblance* between you with your *stern*, strong face and your coal-black hair and this young *Adonis* who looks as if he was made out of *ivory* and rose-petals. Don't flatter yourself, Basil: you are not in the least like him."

"You don't understand me, Henry," answered the artist. "Of course, I am not like him. I know that perfectly well. Indeed, I wouldn't want to

---

reputation, (here) good name
exhibit, show in public
resemblance, likeness
stern, very serious
Adonis, (Greek mythology) a beautiful boy loved by Aphrodite
ivory, hard white substance of elephant (and other) tusks

look like him. There is something *fatal* about all physically and intellectually perfect persons. It is better not to be different from others. You are *noble* and *wealthy*, Harry; I have brains and a talent; Dorian Gray has beauty and we shall all have to pay for what the gods have given us — pay with terrible sufferings."

They walked into the sunny garden and sat down on a bamboo seat.

"Dorian Gray? Is that his name?" asked Lord Henry.

"Yes, that is his name. I didn't want to tell it to you."

"But why not?"

"Oh, I can't explain. When I like people immensely I never tell their names to anyone. It is like giving a part of them to others. You know, I began to love secrets. When I leave *town* now I never tell anyone where I am going. If I did, I would lose all my pleasure. It is a silly habit, I must say, but it seems to bring a great deal of romance into one's life. I suppose you think me awfully foolish."

"Not at all, my dear Basil," answered Lord Henry, "You seem to forget that I am married, and the only charm of marriage is that it makes *deception* absolutely necessary for both parties.

---

fatal, causing death
noble, i.e. a lord
wealthy, rich
town, i.e. London
deception, cheating

I never know where my wife is, and my wife never knows what I am doing. When we meet — and we meet sometimes — we tell each other the most absurd stories with the most serious faces."

"I hate the way you talk about your married life, Harry," said Basil.

"I am afraid I must be going," said Lord Henry, "and before I go I want you to explain to me why you won't exhibit Dorian Gray's picture. I want the real reason."

"I told you the real reason."

"No, you did not. You said it was because there was too much of yourself in it. That is childish."

"Harry," said Basil Hallward, "every portrait that is painted with feeling is a portrait of the artist, not of the *sitter*. It is not the sitter who is revealed by the painter; it is rather the painter who reveals himself. The reason I will not exhibit this picture is that I am afraid that I have shown in it the secret of my own soul."

Lord Henry laughed.

"And what secret is that?" he asked.

"Oh, the story is very simple. There is really very little to tell, Harry," answered the painter, "and I am afraid you will hardly believe it. Two months ago I went to a party at Lady Brandon's. You know, we poor artists have to show ourselves in society from time to time, just to remind the public that we are not savages. Well, after I had been in the room for about ten minutes I suddenly

---

sitter, model

felt that someone was looking at me. I turned halfway round and saw Dorian Gray for the first time. When our eyes met, I realized that I was growing pale. A curious feeling of terror came over me. I knew that I had come face to face with someone whose personality was so fascinating that, if I allowed it to do so, it would *absorb* my whole soul — my art itself. You know how independent I am by nature, Harry. I have always been my own master — till I met Dorian Gray. Then ... but I don't know how to explain it to you. I had a strange feeling that Fate had in store for me *exquisite* joys and exquisite sorrows. I grew afraid

---

absorb, take over
exquisite, very fine

and wanted to leave the room. But at the door I came across Lady Brandon. 'You are not going to run away so soon, Mr Hallward?' she cried out. I could not get rid of her. She led me up to *royalties* and elderly ladies with enormous tiaras and parrot noses. She spoke of me as one of her dearest friends, even though it was only the second time I met her. Suddenly I found myself face to face with the young man whose personality had so strangely excited me. Our eyes met again. I asked Lady Brandon to introduce me to him, but I think we would have spoken to each other even without any introduction. I am sure of that. Dorian told me the same afterwards. He too felt that we were *destined* to know each other."

"And how did Lady Brandon describe this wonderful young man?" asked Lord Henry.

"Oh, something like: 'Charming boy. Quite forgot what he does — oh yes, plays the piano — or is it the violin, dear Mr Gray?' Neither of us could help laughing and we became friends at once."

"Laughter is not at all a bad beginning for a friendship and it is the best ending for it," said the young lord. "Tell me more about Mr Dorian Gray. How often do you see him?"

"Every day. I would be unhappy if I didn't see him every day. He is absolutely necessary to me."

---

royalties, members of the royal family
destined, intended, especially by fate

"How strange! I thought you would never love anything but your art."

"He is all my art now," said the painter *gravely*. "He is much more to me than a model or a sitter. In some curious way ... I wonder if you understand me ... his personality has revealed to me an *entirely* new *manner* in art — an entirely new style. I see things differently, I think of them differently. I can now reflect life in a way that was hidden from me before. This boy — for he seems to me little more than a boy though he is really over 20 — *incarnates* for me the harmony of soul and body!"

"Basil, this is extraordinary! Tell me, is he very fond of you?"

The painter thought for a few moments.

"He likes me," he answered after a pause. "I know he likes me. As a rule, he treats me very well and we sit in the studio and talk of a thousand things. Now and then, however, he seems to enjoy giving me pain. Then I feel that I have given away my whole soul to someone who treats it as if it was a flower to put in his *buttonhole*, a bit of decoration for a summer day."

buttonhole 

---

gravely, very seriously
entirely, completely
manner, style
incarnates, makes real

"I'd like to meet your friend."

"I don't want you to meet him."

"You don't want me to meet him?"

"No."

"Mr Dorian Gray is in the studio, sir," said the butler coming into the garden.

"You must introduce me now," cried Lord Henry laughing.

The painter turned to his servant.

"Ask Mr Gray to wait, Parker. I shall come in a few moments."

The man bowed and went out. Basil looked at Lord Henry.

"Dorian Gray is my dearest friend," he said. "He has a simple and beautiful nature. Don't spoil him. Don't try to influence him. My life as an artist depends on him. Harry, I trust you!"

Chapter 2

As they entered the house they saw Dorian Gray. He was seated at the piano with his back to them turning over the pages of *Schumann*'s "Forest Scenes". When he saw Lord Henry, a faint *blush* coloured his cheeks for a moment and he stood up.

"I beg your pardon, Basil, but I didn't know you had anyone with you."

Schumann, Robert Schumann (1810–56), German composer

blush, reddening of the cheeks as a sign of shame or embarrassment

"This is Lord Henry Wotton, Dorian, an old *Oxford* friend of mine."

Lord Henry stepped forward and they shook hands. Yes, Dorian was certainly extraordinarily handsome, with his red lips, his *frank* blue eyes and curly hair. There was something in his face that made one trust him at once.

Basil Hallward was busy getting his brushes ready. He *hesitated* for a moment and then said, "Harry, I want to finish this picture today. Would you think it awfully rude if I asked you to leave?"

Lord Henry smiled and looked at Dorian Gray.

"Am I to go, Mr Gray?" he asked.

"Oh, please don't, Lord Henry. Basil, if Lord Henry goes, I shall go, too. You never say a word while you are painting and it is horribly *dull* standing on a platform and trying to smile all the time. Ask him to stay. I insist on it."

"Stay, Harry, to please Dorian and to please me," said Hallward, looking at his picture. "It is quite true, I never talk when I am working and never listen either, and it must be dreadfully boring for my sitters. And now, Dorian, get up on the platform and don't move too much or pay any attention to what Lord Henry says. He has a very bad influence over all his friends with the single exception of myself."

Oxford, i.e. Oxford University
frank, honest
hesitate, wait because undecided
dull, boring

Dorian Gray stepped up on the platform with the *air* of a young Greek and smiled to Lord Henry, to whom he had *taken a fancy*. He was so unlike Basil. And he had such a beautiful voice.

"Do you really have a very bad influence, Lord Henry? As bad as Basil says?"

"There is no such thing as a good influence, Mr Gray. Any influence is immoral."

"Why?"

"Because to influence a person is to give him your own soul. He becomes an echo of someone else's music, an actor of a role that was not written for him. The aim of life is self-development. To *realize* one's nature perfectly — that is what each of us lives for. But nowadays people are afraid of themselves. They *deny* pleasures and *suppress* their feelings because of the fear of society or fear of God. The only way to get rid of a temptation is to *yield* to it. And if you try to fight it, your soul will grow sick with longing for the things it has forbidden to itself — with desire for what our monstrous laws have made immoral and unlawful!"

"Stop!" cried Dorian Gray. "You confuse me. I don't know what to say. Don't speak. Let me think. Or rather let me try not to think."

---

air, appearance
take a fancy, to like, often without reason
realize, turn into reality
deny, to not allow
suppress, hide or hold down
yield, to give into

For nearly ten minutes he stood *motionless*, with *parted* lips and eyes strangely bright. He realized that quite new thoughts and feelings were awakening within him. Life suddenly became brightly coloured to him. It seemed to him that he had been walking in fire.

With a smile Lord Henry watched him. He felt strongly interested and amazed at the sudden impression that his words had produced.

"Basil, I am tired of standing," said Dorian Gray suddenly. "I must go out and sit in the garden."

"My dear fellow, I am so sorry. When I am painting, I can't think of anything else. But you stood perfectly still. And I have caught the effect I wanted — the half-parted lips and the bright look in the eyes. I don't know what Harry has been saying to you, but he certainly made you have the most wonderful expression. I suppose he has been giving you *compliments*. You mustn't believe a word that he says."

"He has certainly not been giving me compliments. Perhaps that is the reason that I don't believe anything he has told me!"

"I will go out into the garden with Dorian," said Lord Henry. "It is horribly hot in the studio."

They went out leaving Basil alone with the portrait.

---

motionless, without movement
parted, not closed
compliments, words of praise

"Let us go and sit in the shade," said Lord Henry. "You must not allow yourself to become sunburnt. It will spoil your face and Basil will never paint you again."

"What does it matter?" said Dorian Gray laughing as he sat down on the bench at the end of the garden.

"It should matter everything to you, Mr Gray."

"Why?"

"Because you have the most *marvellous* youth, and youth is the only thing worth having."

"I don't feel that, Lord Henry."

"You don't feel it now. But some day, when you are old and *wrinkled* and ugly, you will feel it, you will feel it terribly. You have a beautiful face, Mr Gray. And beauty is a form of genius — indeed, it is even higher than genius, as it needs no explanations. To me beauty is the wonder of wonders, the true mystery of the world ... Yes, Mr Gray, the gods have been good to you. But what the gods give, they quickly take away. You have only a few years in which to live the perfect and full life. When your youth goes, your beauty will go with it, and then you will suddenly discover that there are no triumphs left for you and the memory of them will make your life even more bitter. You must realize your youth while you have it. Live! Let nothing be lost for you. Always search for new sensations. Be afraid of nothing. There is absolutely nothing in the world but youth!"

---

marvellous, wonderful
wrinkled, with lines in the face

Dorian Gray listened open-eyed and with great attention. Suddenly the painter appeared at the door of the studio and made signs for them to come in.

"I have finished it!" he said. Dorian and Lord Henry looked at each other and smiled.

As they entered the studio, Dorian Gray put his hand on Lord Henry's arm. Lord Henry came up to the picture and examined it. It was certainly a wonderful work of art, and the likeness was amazing.

"My dear fellow, I congratulate you with all my heart," he said. "It is the finest portrait of modern times. Mr Gray, come over and look at yourself."

The young man *started*, as if awakened from some dream.

"Is it really finished?" he muttered, turning towards the picture. When he saw it, he stepped back and his cheeks *flushed* for a moment with pleasure. A look of joy came into his eyes as if he had recognized himself for the first time. The sense of his own beauty came on him like a *revelation*. He had never felt it before. Now, as he stood gazing at his loveliness, he thought of Lord Henry's praise of youth and beauty and his terrible warning of its *brevity*. He felt as if a hand of ice had been laid upon his heart.

"How sad! I shall grow old and ugly and dreadful, but this picture will remain always young. It will never be older than on this summer day. If only it was the other way round! For that I would give everything! I would give my soul for that!"

The painter stared at him in amazement. It was so unlike Dorian to speak like this.

"Yes," he continued, "I know now that when one loses one's good looks one loses everything. Lord Henry is perfectly right. Youth is the only thing worth having. When I see that I am growing old, I shall kill myself."

Hallward turned pale and caught his hand.

"Dorian, don't talk like that. You are not jealous of material things, are you?"

---

start, to move suddenly from rest (NB a common word in Wilde)
flush, to go red
revelation, sudden and great realization
brevity, shortness

"I am jealous of everything whose beauty does not die. I am jealous of the portrait you have painted of me. Why should it keep what I must lose? Every moment that passes takes something from me and gives something to it. Oh, if it were only the other way! If the picture could change and I could be always what I am now. Why did you paint it? It will *mock* me some day — mock me horribly."

The hot tears ran from his eyes; he tore his hand away, threw himself on the divan, and buried his face in the pillows.

"This is your fault, *Harry*," said the painter bitterly.

Lord Henry shrugged his shoulders.

"It is the real Dorian speaking. That is all."

"It is not."

"If it is not, why is it my fault?"

"You should have gone away when I asked you."

"I stayed because you asked me to!"

"Harry, I can't quarrel with my two best friends at once. But both of you have made me hate the finest piece of work I have ever done. I will destroy it. I will not let it come into our three lives and ruin them."

Dorian Gray lifted his golden head from the pillow and looked at Basil walking over to the painting-table. What was he doing there? His

---

mock, to make fun of
Harry, a nickname for 'Henry'

fingers were seeking for something. Yes, it was for the long *palette-knife*. He was going to cut up the canvas!

palette-knife

With a sob the young man leaped from the divan and rushing over to Hallward tore the knife out of his hand.

"Don't, Basil, don't!" he cried. "It would be murder."

"I am glad you like my work at last, Dorian," said the painter coldly when he had recovered from the surprise.

"Like it? I am in love with it. It is part of myself."

"Well, I'll *frame* it and send it to your home. Then you can do with it what you want."

And he walked across the room and rang the bell for tea.

As the door closed behind the guests the painter flung himself down on a sofa and a look of pain came into his face.

---

frame, to put a picture into a frame

Chapter 3

One afternoon, a month later, Dorian Gray was sitting in an arm-chair in the little library of Lord Henry's house talking to Lady Henry. She was a curious woman who tried to look *effective* but looked only untidy.

When Lord Henry at last arrived, he apologized. "So sorry I am late, Dorian," he said, smiling. "I went to buy a piece of old Chinese silk in an antique shop in *Wardour Street* and had to *bargain* for hours for it. Nowadays people know the price of everything and the value of nothing."

"I am afraid I must be going," exclaimed Lady Henry. "Goodbye, Mr Gray, goodbye, Harry. Perhaps I shall see you at Lady Thornbury's?"

And she flew out of the room leaving a slight smell of *jasmine*. Lord Henry lit a cigarette and sat down on the sofa.

"Never marry, Dorian," he said after a pause. "Men marry because they are tired, women because they are curious; both are disappointed."

"I don't think I will ever marry, Henry. I am too much in love. That is one of your *aphorisms*. I am putting it into practice, as with everything that you say."

"Who are you in love with?"

---

effective, producing results
Wardour Street, shopping-street in London
bargain, argue the price
jasmine, climbing plant with white, sweet-smelling flowers
aphorism, a wise saying in a few words

"With an actress," said Dorian Gray blushing.

"Who is she?"

"Her name is Sibyl Vane."

"Never heard of her."

"No one has. But some day everybody will. She is a genius."

"My dear boy, no woman is a genius. Women are a decorative sex. They never have anything to say, but they say it charmingly. There are only five women in London worth talking to, and two of them can't be admitted into *decent society*. However, tell me about your genius. How long have you known her?"

"About three weeks."

"And where did you come across her?"

"I will tell you, Harry, but you mustn't laugh at me. After all, it would never have happened, if I had not met you. I remembered that you said to me on that wonderful evening when we first dined together, that the real secret of happiness is in searching for beauty ... Well, one evening I decided to go out in search of some adventure. I felt that this grey monstrous London must *have* something *in store* for me. I wandered eastward and soon lost my way in a labyrinth of dirty streets and *gloomy* grassless squares. About half past eight I passed by an absurd little theatre with

---

decent society, socially acceptable to the middle-class and above

have in store, to have (sth) ready for future use

gloomy, half-dark

huge *gaudy play-bills*. There was something about them that amused me. You will laugh at me but I went in and paid a whole *guinea* for a *box*. Even now I can't understand why I did so, and yet if I hadn't, I should have missed the greatest romance of my life. I see you are laughing."

"I am not laughing, Dorian, at least I am not laughing at you. But you should not say 'the greatest romance of my life'. You should say 'the first romance of my life'. You will always be loved and you will always be in love with love. This is only the beginning. But I don't want to interrupt you. Go on with your story."

"Well, I found myself in a horrid little private box, with a vulgar curtain in front of me. I began to feel sorry for having come when I noticed the playbill. What do you think the play was, Harry?"

"I think some silly *vaudeville* like 'The Idiot Boy'. Our fathers used to like that sort of play, I believe. But the longer I live, Dorian, the more *keenly* I feel that what was good for our fathers is not good enough for us. In art and in politics our grandfathers are always wrong."

"This play was good enough for us, Harry. It was 'Romeo and Juliet'. I must admit I was rather

---

gaudy, very brightly-coloured
play-bills, poster advertising a play
guinea, in the old money system of pounds, shillings and pence (changed to decimal system in 1972) a guinea was one pound and one shilling
box, i.e. a box at the theatre
vaudeville, kind of theatre entertainment (between 1800 and 1950)
keenly, sharply

sorry for Shakespeare being *staged* in such a hole. Still I felt interested and decided to wait for the first act. At last the curtain rose and the play began. Romeo was a fat elderly gentleman with a *hoarse* voice. But Juliet! Harry, imagine a girl of nearly seventeen years of age with a little flower-like face and a small Greek head with long dark-brown hair; eyes — violet lakes of passion and lips like the petals of a rose. I tell you, Harry, I could hardly see this girl for the mist of tears that came across me. And her voice — I never heard such a voice. You know how a voice can excite. Your voice and the voice of Sibyl Vane are the two things that I shall never forget. When I close my eyes I hear them — each of them says something different. I don't know which to follow. Why should I not love her? She is everything to me. Night after night I go to see her play..."

"Tell me — what are your actual relations with Sibyl Vane?"

Dorian leaped to his feet with flushed cheeks and burning eyes.

"Harry! Sibyl Vane is *sacred*!"

"It is only the sacred things that are worth touching, Dorian," said Lord Henry. "But I am sure she will belong to you some day. When one is in love, one always begins by *deceiving* oneself and one always ends by deceiving others. Are you *acquainted with* her at least?"

---

stage, to put (a play) on stage
hoarse, rough-sounding
sacred, holy
deceive, cheat
acquainted with, to know (each other)

"Of course, I am acquainted with her. I first spoke to her on the third night. She had been playing *Rosalind.* I could not help going to the *wings.* I had thrown her some flowers and she had looked at me — at least I thought that she had. So I asked the director of the theatre to take me to her dressing-room. She was so shy; there is something of a child about her. Her eyes opened wide when I told her what I thought of her performance. I think we were both rather nervous. The director called me 'My Lord', so I assured Sibyl that I was not a lord. She said quite simply to me:

"You look more like a prince. I must call you *Prince Charming.*"

"Upon my word, Dorian, Miss Sibyl knows how to pay compliments."

"You don't understand, Harry. She treated me only as a person in a play. She knows nothing of life. She lives with her mother, an elderly tired woman, who played *Lady Capulet* on the first night and looks as if she *had seen better days.* But Sibyl is absolutely *divine.* Every night I go to see her act and every night she is more wonderful. You laugh, but I tell you she has genius. I love her and I will do everything to make her love me."

Rosalind, the heroine in Shakespeare's comedy, *As You Like It*
wings, side of stage, from where actors make their entrance
Prince Charming, hero of the fairy-tale, *Cinderella*
Lady Capulet, mother of Juliet in Shakespeare's tragedy, *Romeo and Juliet*
had seen better days, i.e. was looking old and ugly
divine, like a god/goddess

Lord Henry watched him with a sense of pleasure. How different he was now from the shy frightened boy he had met in Basil Hallward's studio.

"And what are you going to do about it?" asked Lord Henry.

"I want you and Basil to come with me some night and see her act. You will acknowledge her genius."

"Well, what night shall we go?"

"Let us fix tomorrow. She plays Juliet tomorrow."

"All right. I shall come to the *Bristol* at 8 o'clock and I will get Basil. Will you tell him or shall I write to him?"

"Dear Basil! I have not laid eyes on him for a week. It is rather ungrateful of me as he has sent me my portrait in a wonderful frame, and though I am a little jealous of the picture for being a whole month younger than I am, I must admit that I admire it. Perhaps you had better write to him. I don't want to see him alone. He says things that annoy me. He gives me good advice."

"People are very fond of giving away what they need most of all themselves. Basil puts everything that is charming in him into his work. As a result he has nothing left for life but his *prejudices*, his principles and his common sense."

"I wonder if that is really so, Harry?" said Dorian Gray. "It must be if you say it. And now

---

Bristol, a London theatre

prejudice, pre-judgements, i.e. opinions held before all the facts are known

I have to be off. Sibyl is waiting for me. Don't forget about tomorrow. Goodbye."

When Lord Henry arrived home about half past twelve in the morning he saw a telegram lying on the hall table. He opened it and found it was from Dorian Gray. It told him that he was engaged to be married to Sibyl Vane.

Chapter 4

"Mother, mother, I am so happy!" whispered the girl burying her face on the chest of the faded, tired-looking woman who was sitting in the only armchair that their little dark room contained. "I am so happy!" she repeated, "and you must be happy too!"

Mrs Vane put her thin hands on her daughter's head.

"Happy!" she echoed. "I am only happy, Sibyl, when I see you act. You must not think of anything but your acting. Your director, Mr Isaacs, has been very good to us and we owe him money."

The girl looked up.

"Money, Mother?" she cried. "What does money matter? Love is more than money. We don't need Mr Isaacs any more. Prince Charming rules life for us now." Then she paused. Her cheeks flushed and her lips began to tremble. "I love him," she said dreamily.

"Foolish, foolish child!" repeated her mother.

But the girl did not hear her. She was in the prison of her passion. Her prince, Prince Charming, was with her. His kiss burnt upon her mouth. Her eyelids were warm with his breath.

"Ah, Mother, Mother, let me be happy!" she said at last flinging her arms round her mother's neck and kissing her. Mrs Vane glanced at her and with one of those theatrical gestures that so often become a second nature to actors, took her in her arms.

* * *

"I suppose you have heard the news, Basil?" said Lord Henry that evening as Hallward was shown into a little private room at the Bristol, where dinner had been laid for three.

"No, Harry," answered the artist, giving his hat and coat to the waiter. "What is it? Nothing about politics, I hope? It doesn't interest me. There is hardly a single person in the *House of Commons* worth painting, though many of them need a little *whitewashing*."

"Dorian Gray is engaged to be married," said Lord Henry watching him as he spoke.

Hallward started, and then frowned.

"Impossible!"

"It is perfectly true."

"To whom?"

"To some little actress."

"I can't believe it. Dorian is too sensible for it."

"Dorian is wise enough to do foolish things now and then, my dear Basil."

"But think of Dorian's position and wealth. It would be absurd for him to marry somebody so much beneath him."

"If you want to make him marry this girl, tell him that, Basil, and he is sure to do it then. Whenever a man does a very stupid thing, he always does it from the noblest motives."

"I hope the girl is good, Harry. I don't want to see Dorian tied to some vile creature who may *degrade* his nature and ruin his intellect."

"Oh, she is better than good — she is beautiful," muttered Lord Henry, sipping a glass of *vermouth*. "Dorian says she is beautiful and he is

---

House of Commons, lower house of the UK parliament, to which members are elected
whitewashing, i.e. cleaning away the dirt
degrade, make lower (and lose one's reputation)
vermouth, drink made from wine plus bitter herbs

not often wrong about things of that kind. We are to see her tonight, if that boy doesn't forget about his appointment."

"Are you serious?"

"Quite serious, Basil. I have never been more serious than at the present moment."

"But do you approve of it, Harry?" asked the painter, walking up and down the room and biting his lip. "You can't approve of it — it is some silly *caprice*."

"I never approve or disapprove of anything now. It is an absurd attitude towards life. We are not sent into the world to preach our moral prejudices. You know I am not an *advocate* of marriage. It makes one unselfish — and unselfish people lose their individuality. But there are people whom marriage makes more complex. They keep their *egotism* and add to it many other egos. Besides, every experience is of value, and marriage is certainly an experience. I hope that Dorian Gray will make this girl his wife, passionately adore her for six months and then suddenly become fascinated by someone else. Then he will be a very interesting object for study."

"You don't believe what you say, Harry, you know you don't. If Dorian Gray's life were spoiled, no one would be more sorry than yourself. You are much better than you pretend to be."

Lord Henry laughed.

---

caprice, sudden, often foolish, change of mind or behaviour
advocate, one who speaks in favour of
egotism, selfishness

"I believe everything that I have said. I have the greatest *contempt* for optimism. As for marriage, of course, it is silly. There are other and more interesting bonds between men and women, and I certainly encourage them ... But here is Dorian himself. He will tell you more than I can."

"My dear Harry, my dear Basil, you must both congratulate me!" said Dorian, throwing off his evening *cloak* and shaking each of his friends

cloak

by the hand. "I have never been so happy. Of course, it is sudden, but all really delightful things are sudden. It seems to me that it is the thing I have been looking for all my life." He was flushed with excitement and pleasure and looked extraordinarily handsome.

"I hope you will always be very happy, Dorian," said Hallward, "but I don't quite forgive you for not having let me know of your engagement."

"And I don't forgive you for being late for dinner," said Lord Henry, putting his hand on Dorian's shoulder and smiling. "Come, let us sit down and you will tell us how it all happened."

---

contempt, total lack of respect

"There is really not much to tell," said Dorian, as they took their seats at the small round table. "What happened was simply this. After I left you yesterday evening, Harry, I dressed, had some dinner at a little Italian restaurant and went down to the theatre. Sibyl was playing Rosalind. You should have seen her! When she came on the stage in a boy's clothes she was perfectly wonderful. She had never seemed to me more beautiful. As for her acting — well, you will see her tonight. She is simply a born artist. I forgot that I was in London and in the nineteenth century. I was away with my love in a forest that no man had ever seen. After the performance was over I went to the wings and spoke to her. As we were sitting together, my lips moved towards hers. We kissed each other. I can't describe to you what I felt at that moment. It seemed to me that all my life had concentrated in this wonderful moment. She trembled all over and then flung herself on her knees and kissed my hands."

Lord Henry sipped his champagne in a *meditative* manner.

"At what particular point did you mention the word 'marriage', Dorian? And what did she say in answer? Perhaps you forgot all about it."

"My dear Harry, I did not treat it as a business transaction. I did not make any formal proposal. I told her that I loved her and she said she was not worthy to be my wife. Not worthy! Why, the whole world is nothing to me compared with her."

---

meditative, very thoughtful

"Women are wonderfully practical," murmured Lord Henry, "much more practical than we are. In situations of that kind we often forget to say anything about marriage and they always remind us. I have a theory that it is always the women who propose to us and not we who propose to the women."

Dorian Gray laughed and shook his head.

pedestal

"I love Sibyl Vane. I want to place her on a *pedestal* of gold and to see the world worship the woman who is mine. When I am with her I become different from what you know me to be. I am changed and the mere touch of Sibyl's hand makes me forget you and all your wrong, poisonous, fascinating theories."

"What theories?" asked Lord Henry, helping himself to some salad.

"Oh, your theories about life, your theories about love, your theories about pleasure. All your theories, in fact, Harry."

"Pleasure is the only thing worth making a theory about."

"I know now what pleasure is," said Dorian Gray. "It is to adore someone."

"That is certainly better than being adored," answered Lord Henry, taking some fruits from the plate. "Being adored is a *nuisance*. Women treat us just as mankind treats his gods. They worship us and are always bothering us by asking us to do something for them."

---

nuisance, irritation, unpleasantness

"I think they ask only for what they give us," murmured the young man gravely. "They create love in us and have a right to demand it back."

"That is the trouble. Women, as some witty Frenchman once said, inspire us with the desire to do masterpieces and always prevent us from realizing it."

"Harry, you are dreadful! I don't know why I like you so much."

"You will always like me, Dorian," he replied. "I represent to you all the sins you have never had the courage to commit."

"What nonsense you talk, Harry!" said Dorian. "Let us go down to the theatre. When Sibyl comes on the stage, you will have a new ideal of life. She will represent to you something that you have never known."

"I have known everything," said Lord Henry with a tired look in his eyes, "but I am always ready for a new emotion. Your wonderful girl may thrill me. I love acting. It is much more real than life. Let us go. Dorian, you will come with me. I am so sorry, Basil, but there is only room for two in my carriage. You will have to follow us in a *cab*."

cab

---

cab, horse-drawn taxi

They got up and put on their coats. The painter was silent and gloomy. He did not like this marriage, but it seemed to him to be better than many other things that could happen. A strange sense of loss came over him. He felt that Dorian Gray would never again be to him all that he had been in the past. Life had *stood up* between them ... His eyes darkened and when the cab drew up at the theatre, it seemed to him that he had grown years older.

Chapter 5

For some reason or other the theatre was crowded that night. The young men in the gallery talked to each other across the theatre and shared their oranges with the vulgar girls who sat beside them. Some women were laughing loudly, their voices were horribly shrill and unpleasant.

"What a place to find one's goddess in!" exclaimed Lord Henry.

"Yes," answered Dorian Gray. "It was here I found her, and when she acts, you will forget everything. These common people with rough faces and rude gestures become quite different, when she is on the stage. They sit silently and watch her. They cry and laugh as she wants them to do. She spiritualizes them and then I feel that they are of the same flesh and blood as myself."

---

stand up, become a barrier

"The same flesh and blood! Oh, I hope not!" exclaimed Lord Henry watching the public on the gallery through his opera-glasses.

"Don't pay attention to him, Dorian," said the painter. "I understand what you mean and I believe in this girl. A girl that can do what you describe must be fine and noble. To spiritualize our age — that is something worth doing. This marriage is quite right. I did not think so at first, but I admit it now. The gods made Sibyl Vane for you. Without her your life would be incomplete."

"Thanks, Basil," answered Dorian Gray, pressing his hand. "I knew that you would understand me. Harry is so cynical, he terrifies me. But here is the orchestra. It is quite dreadful, but it will only play for about five minutes. Then the curtain will rise and you will see the girl to whom I am going to give all my life, to whom I have given everything that is good in me."

A quarter of an hour later, among a storm of applause, Sibyl Vane stepped on the stage. Yes, she was certainly lovely — one of the loveliest creatures, Lord Henry thought, that he had ever seen. There was something of the young deer in her shy grace and frightened eyes. She stepped back a few steps and her lips seemed to tremble. Basil Hallward leaped to his feet and began to applaud. Motionless, as if in a dream, Dorian Gray sat gazing at her. Lord Henry looked through his glasses murmuring "Charming! Charming!"

Through the crowd of actors Sibyl Vane moved like a creature from another world. Her body swayed as a reed sways over the water. The curves of her neck were like the curves of a white lily. Yet, she was strangely *indifferent*. Her face

---

indifferent, not interested

showed no sign of joy, when her eyes rested on Romeo. The words she had to speak were spoken in an *artificial* manner. Her voice was beautiful, but from the point of view of intonation it was absolutely false. It took away the life from the verse. It made the passion *insincere*. Dorian Gray grew pale as he watched her. He was shocked and disappointed. Neither of his friends dared to say anything to him. She seemed to them absolutely untalented. Her gestures were absurd. The beautiful monologue of Juliet she recited like a schoolgirl who had been taught to recite by some third-rate teacher. It was not nervousness. It was simply bad art. She was a complete failure.

Even the common, uneducated audience of the gallery lost their interest in the play. They began to talk loudly and to whistle. When the second act was over there came a storm of *hisses*, and Lord Henry got up from his chair and put on his coat.

"She is quite beautiful, Dorian," he said, "but she can't act. Let us go."

"I am going to see the play to the end," answered the young man bitterly. "I am awfully sorry that I have made you waste an evening, Harry. I apologize to you both."

"My dear Dorian, I think Miss Vane is ill," interrupted Hallward. "We will come some other time."

---

artificial, false, unreal
insincere, false, not genuine
hiss, sound made to show dislike (especially at the theatre)

"I wish she were ill," he answered, "but she seems to me simply cold and *callous*. She has quite changed. Last night she was a great artist; this evening she is merely a bad actress."

"Don't talk like that about anyone you love, Dorian. Love is a more wonderful thing than art."

"They are both simply forms of imitation," answered Lord Henry. "But do let us go, Dorian, you must not stay here any longer. And don't look so tragic! The secret of remaining young is never to have an emotion that is *unbecoming*. Besides, I don't suppose you will want your wife to act. So, what does it matter if she plays Juliet like a wooden doll? She is beautiful. What more can you want?"

"Go away, Harry," cried Dorian. "I want to be alone. Can't you see that my heart is breaking?" Hot tears came to his eyes. His lips trembled and he hid his face in his hands.

"Let us go, Basil," said Lord Henry with a strange tenderness in his voice. And the two men went out together.

The last act was played to almost empty benches. The whole play was a fiasco.

As soon as it was over, Dorian Gray rushed behind the stage into the green room. The girl was standing there alone with a look of triumph on her face. Her eyes were lit with bright fire, her parted lips were smiling over some secret of their

---

callous, without feelings
unbecoming, unfitting, unsuitable

own. When he entered, she looked at him and an expression of immense joy came over her.

"How badly I acted tonight, Dorian!" she cried.

"Horribly!" he answered gazing at her in amazement. "Horribly! it was dreadful. Are you ill? You have no idea what I suffered."

The girl smiled. "Dorian, don't you understand?"

"Understand what?" he answered angrily.

"Why I acted so badly tonight. Why I shall never act well again."

He shrugged his shoulders.

"You are ill, I suppose. You shouldn't act when you are ill. My friends were bored. I was bored."

She seemed not to listen to him. She was so happy.

"Dorian, Dorian," she cried, "before I knew you, acting was the only reality of my life. It was only in the theatre that I lived. I thought that it was all true. The joy of *Beatrice* was my joy and the sorrows of *Cordelia* were mine too. I believed in everything. You came — oh, my beautiful love! — and you freed my soul from prison. You taught me what reality really is. Tonight for the first time I realized that the Romeo was *hideous* and old, that the moonlight in the garden was

---

Beatrice, heroine in Shakespeare's comedy, *Much Ado About Nothing*
Cordelia, heroine in Shakespeare's tragedy, *King Lear*
hideous, frightful

false, that the *scenery* was vulgar, and that the words I had to speak were unreal, were not my words, were not what I wanted to say. You had made me understand what love really is. My love! My love! Prince Charming! You are more to me than all art can ever be. Take me away, Dorian, take me away with you, where we can be quite alone. I hate the stage. I could *imitate* a passion that I did not feel but I can't imitate the one that burns me like fire."

Dorian flung himself down on the sofa and turned away his face.

---

scenery, set of painted backgrounds etc. used on a theatre stage
imitate, copy, pretend to have

"You have killed my love," he muttered. Then he leaped up and went to the door. "Yes," he cried, "you have killed my love. You were marvellous because you had genius and intellect, because you realized the dreams of great poets. You have thrown it all away. You are ordinary and stupid. Without your art you are nothing. My God! How madly I was in love with you! What a fool I have been! You are nothing to me now. I will never see you again."

The girl grew white and trembled. She flung herself at his feet and lay there like a faded flower.

"Dorian, Dorian, don't leave me!" she whispered. "I am so sorry I didn't act well. I was thinking of you all the time. But I will try — indeed, I will try. Don't be cruel to me because I love you more than anything in the world."

She lay on the floor like a wounded animal and Dorian with his beautiful eyes looked down at her with contempt. There is always something strange about the emotions of people whom one has stopped loving. Sibyl Vane seemed to him absurdly melodramatic. Her tears and sobs annoyed him.

"I am going," he said at last in his calm, clear voice. "I don't wish to be unkind but I can't see you again. You have disappointed me."

He turned and left the room. In a few moments he was out of the theatre.

He took a cab and drove home. As he passed through the library towards the door of his bed-

room, his eye fell upon the portrait Basil Hallward had painted of him. He stepped back as if in surprise. But after some time he went over to the picture and examined it. In the dim light of the room it seemed to him that the face had changed. The expression was different. There was a touch of *cruelty* round the mouth. It was certainly strange. What did it mean?

He threw himself into a chair and began to think. Suddenly he remembered what he had said in Basil Hallward's studio the day the portrait had been finished. Yes, he remembered it perfectly. He had expressed a mad wish that he himself might remain young, and the picture grow old reflecting all his passions and sins. But his wish

---

cruelty, desire to cause pain and suffering

could not have been realized! Such things were impossible. It seemed monstrous even to think of them. But there was the picture before him with the touch of cruelty round the mouth. Cruelty! Had he been cruel? It was the girl's fault, not his. He had dreamed of her as a great actress but she disappointed him. And yet, a feeling of regret came over him as he thought of her lying at his feet sobbing like a little child. Yes, he would go back to Sibyl Vane, marry her, try to love her again. It was his duty to do so. She must have suffered more than he had. Poor child! He had been selfish and cruel to her. They would be happy together. His life with her would be beautiful and pure. He would not see Lord Henry any more, never again listen to his poisonous theories.

He got up from his chair and, glancing at the portrait again, he *shuddered*. "How horrible!" he murmured to himself. Then he took a high screen and put it in front of the picture.

Chapter 6

It was long past noon when he awoke. As soon as he dressed he went into the library and sat down to a light breakfast. It was a beautiful day and he felt perfectly happy.

Suddenly his eye fell on the screen that he had placed in front of the portrait and he started.

---

shuddered, to shake with fear or horror

"Is Monsieur cold?" asked his servant putting an omelette on the table. "Shall I shut the window?"

Dorian shook his head.

"I am not cold," he murmured.

Was it all true? Had the portrait really changed? Or had it been simply his own imagination that had made him see a look of evil where there had been a look of joy? Surely a painted canvas could not *alter*. It was absurd.

He got up and locked the doors. Then he drew the screen aside and saw himself face to face. It was perfectly true. The portrait had altered. He shuddered and going back to the sofa lay there gazing at the picture in horror.

However, he felt that it had done one thing for him. It made him realize how *unjust*, how cruel he had been to Sibyl Vane. But it was not too late to make it good again. She could still be his wife. His selfish love would be transformed into a nobler passion and the portrait would be to him a guide through life. It would be his conscience, an ever-present proof that man is able to ruin his soul.

He went over to the table and wrote a passionate letter to the girl he had loved, begging her forgiveness and accusing himself of madness. There is a kind of pleasure in *self-reproach*. When we blame ourselves, we feel that no one else has

---

alter, change
unjust, unfair
self-reproach, giving oneself the blame

a right to blame us. When Dorian had finished the letter he felt that he had been forgiven.

There was a knock at the door and he heard Lord Henry's voice outside.

"My dear boy, I must see you. Let me come in. I can't bear your shutting yourself up like this."

Dorian Gray made no answer at first but remained quite still. The knocking continued and grew louder. Yes, it was better to let Lord Henry in, to explain to him the new life he was going to lead, and to break with him if necessary. He jumped up, pulled the screen quickly in front of the picture and unlocked the door.

"I am so sorry, Dorian," said Lord Henry as he entered. "But you must not think too much about it."

"You mean Sibyl Vane?" asked the youth.

"Yes, of course," answered Lord Henry. "It is dreadful, but it was not your fault. Tell me, did you go behind the stage and see her after the play was over?"

"Yes."

"I was sure you did. Did you quarrel with her?"

"I was brutal, Harry, perfectly brutal. But it is all right now. I want to be good. I shall marry Sibyl."

"Marry Sibyl?" said Lord Henry in amazement. "But, my dear Dorian ... you know nothing then?"

"What do you mean?"

Lord Henry took Dorian Gray's hands in his own and held them tightly.

"Sibyl is dead."

A cry of pain broke from the young man's lips.

"Dead! Sibyl dead! It is not true!"

"It is quite true, Dorian," said Lord Henry sadly. "It is in all the morning papers. There will be an *inquiry*, of course, and you must not be mixed up in it. I suppose they don't know your name at the theatre? If they don't, it is all right. Did anyone see you going round to her room?"

Dorian did not answer for a few moments. Finally he murmured:

"Harry, did you say 'inquiry'? What do you mean by that? Did Sibyl...? Oh, Harry, I can't bear it! Be quick. Tell me everything at once."

"I have no doubt it was an accident, Dorian, though the public must think it was a suicide. It seems that she was leaving the theatre with her mother at about half past twelve. She said she had forgotten something upstairs. They waited some time for her but she did not come down again. Then they found her lying dead on the floor of her dressing-room. She had swallowed something — some dreadful thing they use at theatres. I don't know what it was but I think it was *prussic acid*, as she seems to have died at once."

"Harry, Harry, it is terrible!" cried Dorian. "I have killed Sibyl Vane. Oh, Harry, how I loved her once! It seems years ago to me now. She was everything to me. Then came that dreadful night — was it really only last night? — when she

---

inquiry, police investigation
prussic acid, very poisonous acid that quickly causes death

acted so badly and my heart almost broke. She explained it all to me. It was terribly pathetic but I was not moved a bit. Suddenly something happened that made me afraid. I can't tell you what it was but it was terrible. I said I would go back to her. I said I felt I had done wrong. And now she is dead and there is nothing to keep me straight. She had no right to kill herself."

"Do you remember what you said to me the day before yesterday? I see now it was absolutely true and it is the key to everything."

"What was that, Harry?"

"You said that Sibyl Vane represented to you all the heroines of the play — that she was *Desdemona* one night and Ophelia the other; that if she died as Juliet she came to life as Rosalind."

"She will never come to life again now," muttered Dorian, burying his face in his hands.

"No, she will never come to life. She has played her last part."

There was a silence. The evening crept into the room. The colours faded out of things. After some time Dorian Gray looked up at Lord Henry.

"No one has ever understood me as you have."

"We are only at the beginning of our friendship, Dorian," answered Lord Henry shaking him by the hand. "Perhaps I shall see you at the Opera tonight. Goodbye. Remember, Patti is singing."

As he closed the door behind him, Dorian Gray turned to the screen and drew it back. No, there was no further change in the picture. It had

---

Desdemona, heroine in Shakespeare's tragedy, *Othello*

received the news of Sibyl Vane's death before he had known of it himself. The expression of cruelty that deformed the fine lines of the mouth, no doubt, appeared at the moment when the girl drank the poison.

Poor Sibyl. She died for love of him, and love would always be sacred to him now. He looked again at the picture. He felt that the time had really come for making his choice. Eternal youth, passions, pleasures, wild joys and still wilder sins — he would have all these things. The portrait could bear the burden of his shame. If the picture was to alter, it was to alter. There would be real pleasure in watching it. This portrait would be to him the most magical of mirrors. As it had revealed to him his own body, it would reveal to him his own soul.

He drew the screen back into its former place in front of the picture, smiling as he did so, and passed into the bedroom to dress. An hour later he was at the Opera and Lord Henry was leaning over his chair.

Chapter 7

As Dorian was sitting down to breakfast next morning, Basil Hallward arrived.

"I am so glad I have found you, Dorian," he said gravely. "I called last night and they told me you were at the Opera. Of course, I knew that was impossible. But I wish you had informed me where you had really gone. I passed a dreadful evening afraid that one tragedy might be followed by another. I read about Sibyl's death quite by chance in a newspaper. I can't tell you how heart-broken I am about the whole thing. I know how you must suffer. But where were you? Did you go down to see the girl's mother? Poor woman! What a state she must be in! And her only child! What did she say about it all?"

"My dear Basil," murmured Dorian Gray. "I was at the Opera. You should have come there. I met Lady Gwendolen, Harry's sister, for the first time. She is perfectly charming and Patti sang divinely. Don't talk about horrid things. If one doesn't talk about a thing, it has never happened."

"You went to the Opera?" said Hallward, speaking very slowly and with a touch of pain in his voice. "You went to the Opera while Sibyl Vane was lying dead, not even buried!"

"Stop, Basil! I don't want to hear it," cried Dorian leaping to his feet. "You must not tell me about these things. What is done is done. It is in the past."

"Dorian, this is horrible! Something has changed you completely. You were the most unspoiled creature in the whole world. I don't know what has come over you. You talk as if you had no heart, no pity in you. It is all Harry's influence. I see that."

Dorian went over to the window and looked out for a few moments on the green garden lit by the sun.

"I owe a great deal to Harry, Basil," he said at last, "more than I owe to you. I don't know what you want. What do you want?"

"I want the Dorian Gray I used to paint," said the artist sadly.

"Basil," said Dorian going over to him and putting his hand on his shoulder, "you have come too late. Yesterday when I heard that Sibyl Vane had killed herself..."

"Killed herself? Good Heavens! Is that what happened?" cried Hallward, looking up at him with an expression of horror.

"My dear Basil! Surely you don't think it was an accident. Of course, she killed herself."

"How terrible!" said Hallward.

"No," said Dorian Gray, "there is nothing terrible about it. Sibyl was always a heroine. The last night — the night you saw her — she acted badly because she had known the reality of love and could not imitate it on stage. There is nothing more to be said."

The painter was silent.

"Well, Dorian," he said at last with a sad smile. "I won't speak to you again about this horrible thing after today. I only hope your name won't be mentioned in connection with it. The inquiry is to take place this afternoon. Do they know your name?"

Dorian shook his head and a look of *annoyance* passed over his face at the mention of the word "inquiry".

---

annoyance, irritation

"They don't know my name," he answered.

"But surely she did?"

"Only my Christian name and I am quite sure she never mentioned it to anyone. She told me once that they were all rather curious to learn who I was, and that she always told them my name was Prince Charming. It was nice of her. You must do me a drawing of Sibyl, Basil. I should like to have something more of her than the memory of a few kisses and some *pathetic* words."

"I will try to do something, Dorian, if it can please you. But you yourself must come and sit for me again. I can't get on without you."

"I will never sit for you again, Basil. It is impossible!" Dorian exclaimed, stepping back.

The painter stared at him.

"My dear boy, what nonsense!" he cried. "Are you saying that you don't like the portrait? Where is it? Why have you put the screen in front of it? Let me look at it. It is the best thing I have ever done."

Hallward walked towards the corner of the room, but a cry of terror broke from Dorian's lips and he rushed between the painter and the screen.

"Basil," he said looking very pale, "you must not look at it. I don't wish you to."

"Not look at my own work? You are not serious. Why shouldn't I look at it?" exclaimed Hallward.

---

pathetic, (here) useless

"If you try to look at it, Basil, I swear I will never speak to you again as long as I live. I am quite serious. I am not going to explain and don't ask me why. But remember, if you touch the screen, everything is over between us."

Hallward was *thunderstruck*. He looked at Dorian Gray in absolute amazement. He had never seen him like this before. His eyes were like disks of blue fire. He was trembling all over.

"Dorian!"

"Don't speak!"

"But what is the matter? Of course I won't look at it if you don't want me to," he said rather coldly, turning on his heels and going to the door. "But will you sit for me again?"

"No! I can't explain it to you, Basil, but I will never sit for you again. There is something fatal about every portrait. It has a life of its own. I will come and have tea with you. That will be just as pleasant."

"Pleasanter for you, I am afraid," murmured Hallward sadly. So, goodbye. I am sorry you won't let me look at the picture once again. But that can't be helped. I quite understand how you feel about it."

As he left the room, Dorian Gray thought to himself. Poor Basil! How little he knew of the true reason. He sighed and touched the bell. The portrait must be hidden away *at all costs*. He could not risk his secret being discovered. He was mad

---

thunderstruck, extremely surprised
at all costs, whatever the trouble it takes

to leave the portrait in a room where any of his friends could come in.

* * *

When the servant entered, he asked him to tell the housekeeper that he wanted to see her and that she was to bring all her keys. After a few moments Mrs Leaf appeared in the library. He asked her for the key to the schoolroom.

"The old schoolroom, Mr Dorian?" she exclaimed. "Why, it is full of dust. It is not fit for you to see, sir. It hasn't been opened for nearly five years, not since his lordship died."

He winced at the mention of his grandfather. He had hateful memories of him.

"That does not matter," he answered. "I simply want to see the place — that is all. Give me the key."

"Here is the key," said the old lady giving it to him with trembling hands. "But you're not thinking of living up there, sir?"

"No, no," he cried in annoyance. "Thank you, Mrs Leaf. You may go."

As the door behind her closed, Dorian put the key in his pocket and looked round the room. His eye fell on a large red satin coverlet embroidered with gold. Yes, that would serve to wrap around the dreadful thing. For a moment he regretted that he had not told Basil the true reason why he had wished to hide the picture away. But it was too late now. He took up from the sofa the big red-and-gold coverlet and draped it over the portrait.

Then he called the servants and told them to take the picture away. He followed them up the stairs to the schoolroom, which he had not entered for more than four years. He had used it as a playroom when he was a child. Several moments from his childhood came back to him as he looked around. He *recalled* the innocence of his boyhood, and it seemed horrible to him that it was here that the portrait had to be hidden away. How little he had thought in those faraway days of all that was in store for him!

But there was no other place in the house so secure from curious eyes as this. He had the key and no one else could enter it. Beneath its red coverlet the face painted on the canvas could

---

recall, to remember

grow old and cruel. What did it matter? No one could see it. He himself would not see it. Why should he watch the corruption of his soul? He would keep his youth — that was enough. And besides, couldn't he get better after all? Some love might come across his life and *purify* him. Perhaps some day the cruel look would pass away from the *sensitive* mouth and he would show to the world Basil Hallward's masterpiece.

When the sound of the footsteps of the servants had died away, Dorian locked the door and put the key in his pocket. He felt safe now. No one would ever look at the horrible thing. No eye but his would ever see his shame.

On reaching the library he found a note from Lord Henry. Beside it, was a book wrapped in yellow paper and a copy of the *St James's Gazette* placed on the tea-tray. The note simply said that Lord Henry would be at *the club* at 8.15. He opened the newspaper and looked through it. A red-pencil mark on the fifth page caught his eye. It drew attention to the following paragraph: "Inquiry of an Actress. — An inquiry was held this morning at the Bell Tavern by Mr Danby, the District *Coroner*, on the body of Sibyl Vane, a

---

purify, make (his soul) clean
sensitive, full of feeling
St James's Gazette, London newspaper
the club, upper-class men were often members of various men-only clubs in London
Coroner, public official who holds an inquiry into a person's death

young actress who played at the Royal Theatre. A verdict of death by accident was confirmed. A great sympathy was expressed to the mother of the girl who is still in shock."

Dorian frowned, tore the paper in two and threw the pieces away. How ugly it all was. He was angry with Lord Henry for having sent him the report. And it was certainly stupid of him to have marked it with red pencil. His servant might have read it. The man knew more than enough English for that.

His eye fell on the yellow book that Lord Henry had sent him. What was it? he wondered. He flung himself into an arm-chair and began to turn over the pages. After a few minutes he became fascinated. It was the strangest book that he had ever read. Things that he had dimly dreamed of were suddenly made real to him. Things of which he had never dreamed were now revealed before him.

It was a novel without a plot, simply a story of a young *Parisian* who spent his life trying to relive all the passions and thoughts of the past centuries in order to experience everything in the world.

It was almost nine o'clock before Dorian reached the club, where he found Lord Henry sitting alone and looking very bored.

"I am so sorry, Harry," he exclaimed, "but it is your fault. That book you sent me so fascinated me that I forgot how the time was passing."

Parisian, person from Paris

"Yes, I was sure you would like it," replied Lord Henry, rising from the chair.

"I didn't say I liked it, Harry. I said it fascinated me. That is a great difference."

"Ah, you have discovered that?" muttered Lord Henry.

And they passed into the dining-room.

Chapter 8

For years Dorian Gray could not free himself from the influence of the book. Or, perhaps, he never wanted to free himself from it. The hero, the wonderful young Parisian in whom romanticism and the brain of a scientist were so strangely mixed, seemed to him a model of himself. And the whole book seemed to him to contain the story of his own life written before he had lived it.

But in one point he was more fortunate than the novel's hero. He never knew the fear of mirrors that the young Parisian knew when he realized he had lost his beauty. Because the wonderful beauty that had so fascinated Basil Hallward and many others never left Dorian. Even those who heard the most dreadful things about him could not believe any evil rumours when they saw him. Men who talked loudly became silent, when Dorian Gray entered the room. There was such purity in his face that they became ashamed. They wondered how he could keep his charm and innocence.

There were many young people who saw in Dorian Gray the true realization of an ideal of which they had often dreamed in *Eton* or Oxford days. They tried to imitate his manner of dressing and the fashions that he followed from time to time. But he himself desired to be more than a mere model of fashion. He wanted to create a new philosophy of life, his own principles of New *Hedonism*.

Often on returning home he crept upstairs to the locked room, opened the door with the key that never left him now and stood with a mirror in front of the portrait looking at the evil and aging face on the canvas and at the fair young face that laughed at him from the mirror. The striking contrast gave him pleasure. He fell more and more in love with his own beauty and became more and more interested in the corruption of his own soul.

True, there were moments at night when, lying sleepless in his bedroom or sitting in dirty taverns under a false name and in disguise, he thought that he had ruined his soul. But such moments were rare. That curiosity about life, which Lord Henry had first excited in him as they sat together in the garden of their friend, seemed to increase with time. The more he knew, the more he desired to know. Dorian Gray had been poisoned by the book. There were moments

---

Eton, famous English private school
Hedonism, the philosophy of living life purely for pleasure

when he looked on evil simply as a way through which he could realize his own idea of the beautiful.

* * *

It was on the ninth of November, the eve of his thirty-eighth birthday, as he often remembered afterwards. He was walking home at about eleven o'clock from Lord Henry's, where he had had supper. He was dressed in a heavy fur coat, as the night was cold and foggy. At the corner of Grosvenor Square and South Audley Street a man passed him in the mist walking very fast and with the collar of his grey coat turned up. He had a bag in his hand. Dorian recognized him. It was Basil Hallward. A strange sense of fear came over him. He made no sign of recognition and went on quickly in the direction of his house. But Hallward recognized him. He hurried after him and in a few moments his hand was on his arm.

"Dorian! What extraordinary luck! I was waiting for you in your library since nine o'clock. I am going to Paris on the midnight train and wanted to see you before I left. Didn't you recognize me?"

"In this fog, my dear Basil? Why, I can't even recognize Grosvenor Square. I am sorry you are going away, as I have not seen you for ages. But I suppose you will be back soon?"

"No, I am going to be out of England for six months. I intend to take a studio in Paris and shut myself up till I finish a great picture I have in my head. However, it wasn't about myself I wanted to talk. Here we are at your door. Let me come in for a moment. I have something to say to you."

"I shall be delighted, but won't you miss your train?" said Dorian Gray slowly as he passed up the steps and opened the door. Hallward looked at his watch.

"I have plenty of time," he answered. "The train leaves at 12.15 and it is only eleven now. In fact, I was on my way to the club to look for you when I met you. I have already sent off my luggage. All I have with me is in this bag and I can easily get to Victoria in twenty minutes."

Dorian looked at him and smiled.

"What a way for a famous painter to travel! A handbag and a light coat. Come in or the fog will get into the house. And please don't talk about anything serious. Nothing is serious nowadays. At least nothing should be."

Hallward shook his head as he entered and followed Dorian into the library. He took his cap and coat off and threw them on the bag that he had placed in the corner.

"But, my dear fellow, I want to speak to you seriously. Don't frown like that. You make it so much more difficult for me."

"What do you want to talk about?" cried Dorian flinging himself down on the sofa. "I hope it is not about myself. I am tired of myself tonight. I want to be somebody else."

"It is about yourself," answered Hallward in his grave, deep voice, "and I must say it to you. I shall only keep you half an hour."

Dorian sighed and lit a cigarette.

"Half an hour!" he murmured.

"It is not much to ask of you, Dorian, and it is entirely for your own sake that I am speaking. I think you should know that the most dreadful things are said against you in London."

"I don't wish to know anything about them. I love scandals about other people but scandals about myself don't interest me."

"They must interest you, Dorian. Every gentleman is interested in his good name. Mind you, I don't believe these rumours at all. At least I can't believe them when I see you. Sin is a thing that writes itself across a man's face. It cannot be hidden. But I see you very seldom. You never come down to the studio now and when I am away from you and hear all these hideous things that people are whispering about you, I don't know what to say. Why is it, Dorian, that so many gentlemen in London will neither go to your house nor invite you to theirs? Why is your friendship so fatal to young men?"

"Stop, Basil. You are talking about things of which you know nothing," said Dorian Gray, biting his lip and with a note of contempt in his voice. "You ask me about these young men. Did I teach them their *vices*? I know how people *slander* in England. In this country it is enough for a man to have money and brains for every evil tongue to gossip about him. What sort of lives do these

---

vice, evil behaviour (opposite of 'virtue')
slander, to hurt by making a false statement

people who pretend to moral lead themselves? My dear fellow, you forget that we live in the land of *hypocrites.*"

"Dorian," cried Hallward, "that is not the question. England is bad enough, I know, and English society is all wrong. That is the reason why I want you to be good. You have not been good. We have a right to judge a man by the influence he has over his friends. Your friends have lost all sense of honour, of goodness, of purity. You have filled them with a mad *lust* for pleasure. They have gone down into the depths. You led them there. Yes, you led them there and you can smile as you are smiling now. And there is something worse. I know you and Harry are friends. At least for that reason you should not have made his sister's name a byword."

"Stop, Basil. You have gone too far."

"I must speak and you must listen. When you met Lady Gwendolen, nobody could say a bad word about her. And now? Will any decent woman take a risk to appear with her in public? Even her children were not allowed to live with her. And this is not all. There are other stories — peole saw you creeping at dawn out of the most dreadful *dens* in London. Can they be true? When I first heard them I laughed. But now I hear them all the time and they make me shudder. Let your

---

hypocrite, person who says one thing (positive) but does another (negative)
lust, very strong desire (often sexual)
den, place of secret, especially unlawful activity.

influence be for good, not for evil. They say that you corrupt everyone with whom you become friends, that when you enter a house you bring shame to this house. I don't know whether it is so or not. Before I can answer that I have to see your soul."

"To see my soul!" muttered Dorian Gray leaping from the sofa and turning almost white from fear.

"Yes," answered Hallward gravely and with deep sorrow in his voice. "To see your soul. But only God can do that."

A bitter laugh broke from the lips of the younger man.

"You shall see it yourself tonight!" he cried, taking a lamp from the table. "Come on, it is your own work. Why shouldn't you look at it? You can tell the world all about it afterwards if you like. Nobody will believe you, and if they believe you they will like me even more for it. You have chattered enough about moral corruption. Now you shall look at it face to face."

Dorian felt a terrible joy at the thought that someone would share his secret and that the man who had painted the portrait that was the origin of all his shame, would have the hideous memory of what he had done for the rest of his life.

"Yes," he continued coming close to him and looking into his eyes. "I shall show you my soul. You shall see the thing that you think only God can see."

Hallward stepped back.

"This is horrible, Dorian. You must not say things like these. You must give me some answer to these terrible accusations that are made against you. If you tell me that they are absolutely untrue from beginning to end, I shall believe you. Deny them, Dorian, deny them!"

Dorian Gray smiled.

"Come upstairs, Basil," he said quietly. "I keep a diary of my life from day to day. I shall show it to you."

"I shall come with you, Dorian, if you wish it. I see I have missed my train, but that does not matter. I can go tomorrow. All I want is a plain answer to my question."

"It shall be given to you upstairs."

Chapter 9

Dorian Gray walked up the stairs with Basil Hallward behind him. The lamp cast fantastic shadows on the walls and staircase.

When they reached the top *landing* Dorian put the lamp down on the floor and taking out the key turned it in the lock.

"You insist on knowing, Basil?" he asked in a low voice.

"Yes."

"I am delighted," he answered smiling. "You are the only man in the world who has a right to know everything about me."

---

landing, flat space between two sets of stairs

Taking up the lamp he opened the door and went in.

"Shut the door behind you," he whispered, as he placed the lamp on the table.

Hallward glanced round him with a *puzzled* expression. The room looked as if it had not been lived in for years. As Dorian was lighting a half-burned candle that was standing on the *mantle-piece*, he saw that the whole place was covered with dust and that the carpet was in holes. A mouse ran across the floor. There was a smell of *mould*.

mantlepiece

"So you think that it is only God who sees the soul, Basil? Draw the curtain back and you will see mine."

His voice was cold and stern.

"You are mad, Dorian, or playing a part," muttered Hallward frowning.

"You won't? Then I must do it myself," said the younger man and he tore the coverlet away and flung it on the ground.

An exclamation of horror broke from the painter's lips as he saw in the dim light the hideous face on the canvas grinning at him.

---

puzzled, confused, unknowing
mould, soft, greenish growth on walls (and some foods)

Good heavens! It was Dorian Gray's own face that he was looking at! The hideous expression had not yet entirely spoiled that marvellous beauty. There was still some gold in the thinning hair and the mouth was still *sensual*. Yes, it was Dorian himself. But who had done it? He recognized his own brush and the frame was his own design. The idea was monstrous, yet he felt afraid. He took the lighted candle and held it to the picture.

In the left-hand corner was his own name.

It was some dreadful *parody* — and yet it was his own picture! He knew it and he felt as if his

---

sensual, physically, especially sexually attractive
parody, copy intending to amuse or hurt

blood had changed in a moment from fire to ice. His own picture! What did it mean? Why had it changed?

He turned and looked at Dorian Gray with the eyes of a sick man. The young man was watching him with that strange expression that can be seen on the faces of those who are absorbed in a play when some great artist is acting. He had taken a flower out of his buttonhole and was smelling it.

"What does this mean?" cried out Hallward at last.

Dorian did not take off his eyes off the painter.

"Years ago when I was almost a boy, you met me, flattered me and taught me to be proud of my good looks. One day you introduced me to a friend of yours, who explained to me the wonder of youth. And you finished the portrait of me that revealed to me the wonder of beauty. In a mad moment that even now I don't know whether I regret or not, I made a wish, perhaps you would call it a prayer ..."

"I remember it! But you told me you had destroyed the picture."

"That is wrong. It has destroyed me."

"I don't believe it is my picture. This is the face of a *satyr*."

"It is the face of my soul."

"It has the eyes of a devil."

---

satyr, (Greek mythology) a god represented as half man, half goat

"Each of us has heaven and hell in him, Basil," said Dorian.

Hallward turned again to the portrait and gazed at it.

"My God! If it is true," he exclaimed, "and this is what you have done with your life, you must be even worse than people think."

His hand shook and the candle fell on the floor. He flung himself into the armchair by the table and buried his face in his hands.

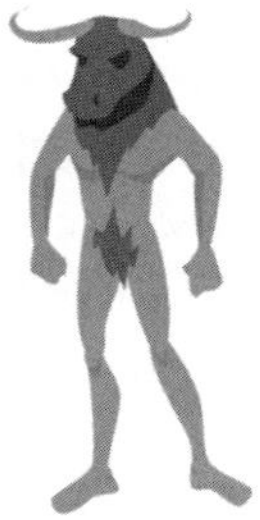

satyr

"Good God, Dorian, what a lesson! What an awful lesson!"

There was no answer, but he could hear the man sobbing at the window.

"Pray, Dorian, pray," he murmured. "Let us pray together. I *worshipped* you too much. We are both punished."

Dorian Gray turned slowly around and looked at him with eyes full of tears.

---

worship, to show great honour to (especially a god)

"It is too late, Basil," he said.

"It is never too late, Dorian. You have done enough evil in your life. My God! Don't you see that damned portrait grinning at us?"

Dorian Gray glanced at the picture and suddenly an uncontrollable feeling of hatred for Basil Hallward came over him, as if his portrait

on the canvas was whispering into his ear. The mad *fury* of a hunted animal arose within him. He hated the man who was sitting at the table more than he had ever hated anything in his whole life.

---

fury, great anger

He glanced around the room. His eye fell on the knife that he had used some days before to cut a piece of cord. He moved slowly towards it, passing Hallward. As soon as he got behind him he seized the knife and turned round. Hallward tried to rise in his chair but Dorian rushed at him and dug the knife into the *artery* behind his ear. Pressing the man's head down on the table he stabbed again and again.

Hallward gave a terrible cry and threw up his arms. Dorian stabbed him twice more, but the man did not move. Something began to drip on the carpet. He waited for a moment, still pressing the head, and listened. The house was absolutely quiet. No one was nearby. He took out the key and locked himself inside.

He felt strangely calm, and walking over to the window opened it and stepped out on the balcony. He looked down and saw the policeman *making his rounds*. A strong wind shook the black leafless branches of the trees. He *shivered* and went back, closing the window behind him. He could not help seeing the dead man. How still he was, how horribly white the long hands looked. It was like a dreadful wax figure.

Having locked the door behind him he crept quietly downstairs. The wooden steps seemed to cry out as if in pain. He stopped several times and

---

artery, tube that carries blood from heart to rest of body
make rounds, walk round on regular patrol
shiver, to shake with cold or fear

waited. No, everything was still. It was merely the sound of his own footsteps. When he reached the library he saw Basil's bag and coat in the corner. They must be hidden away somewhere, he thought. He unlocked a secret wall-cabinet in which he kept his own *curious disguises* and put them into it. He could easily burn them afterwards. Then he pulled out his watch. It was twenty minutes to two in the morning.

He sat down and began to think ... What evidence was there against him?

Basil Hallward had left the house at eleven. No one had seen him come in again. Most of the servants had gone to bed ... Paris! Yes. It was to Paris that Basil had gone and by the midnight train as he had intended. Months will pass before any suspicions will arise. Months! Everything can be destroyed long before then.

A sudden thought struck him. He put on his fur coat and hat and went out into the hall. He unlocked the door and slipped out, shutting the door very gently behind him. Then he began ringing the bell. In about five minutes his servant appeared, half dressed and looking very sleepy.

"I am sorry I had to wake you up, Francis," he said stepping in, "but I had forgotten my key. What time is it?"

"Ten minutes past two, sir," answered the man looking at the clock.

"Ten minutes past two? How horribly late! You must wake me at nine tomorrow. I have some work to do."

---

curious disguises, i.e. to hide his identity

"All right, sir."

"Did anyone call this evening?"

"Mr Hallward, sir. He stayed here till eleven and then he went away to catch his train."

"Oh, I am sorry I didn't see him. Did he leave any message?"

"No, sir, except that he will write to you from Paris if he does not find you at the club."

"All right, Francis. Don't forget to call me at nine tomorrow."

"No, sir."

The man went down the passage in his slippers. Dorian Gray threw his hat and coat upon the table and passed into the library. For a quarter of an hour he walked up and down the room, biting his lip and thinking. Then he took the Address Book from one of the shelves and began to turn over the leaves. "Alan Campbell, 152 Hertford Street." Yes, that was the man he wanted.

Chapter 10

At nine o'clock the next morning his servant came in to Dorian's bedroom with a cup of chocolate on a tray and opened the *shutters*. Dorian was sleeping quite peacefully lying on his right side with one hand under his cheek. He looked like a boy who had been tired with play or study. The man had to touch him twice on the shoulder before he woke and as he opened his eyes, a faint

shutters

smile passed across his lips as though he had been in some delightful dream.

He turned round and began to sip his chocolate. The November sun came streaming into the room. The sky was cloudless and the air was warm. It was almost like a morning in May. Gradually the events of the last night crept into his brain and for a moment the same curious feeling of hatred for Basil Hallward came back to him. The dead man was still sitting in the library and in the sunlight now. How horrible that was! Such hideous things were for the darkness, not for the day.

After breakfast Dorian wrote two letters. One he put in his pocket, the other he gave to his servant.

"Take this letter to 152 Hertford Street, Francis, to Mr Campbell."

As soon as he was alone, he lit a cigarette and began drawing: first flowers and houses and then human faces. Suddenly he noticed that every face that he drew had a fantastic likeness to Basil Hallward. He frowned and getting up went over to the bookcase and took a book. He stretched himself on the sofa and tried to read, but could not. A horrible terror came over him. What if Alan Campbell was out of England? Days would pass before he could come back. Perhaps he would refuse to come. What would he do then? Every moment was of vital importance. They had been great friends once, five years before. Then the friendship came suddenly to an end. When they met *in society* now, it was only Dorian Gray who smiled; Alan Campbell never did.

The suspense became unbearable — but at last the door opened and his servant entered.

"Mr Campbell, sir," said the man.

A sigh of relief broke from Dorian's lips and the colour came back to his cheeks.

"Ask him to come in at once, Francis." He felt that he was himself again.

In a few moments Alan Campbell walked in looking rather *pale* especially in contrast to his black hair and dark eyebrows.

"Alan! This is kind of you. I thank you for coming."

"I had intended never to enter your house again, Gray. But you said it was a matter of life and death." His voice was hard and cold. There was contempt in his eyes that he turned on Dorian. He kept his hands in the pockets of his coat and seemed not to notice the hand that Dorian held out to him.

"Yes, it is a matter of life and death, Alan, and not only for me. Sit down."

Campbell took a chair by the table and Dorian sat opposite to him. The two men's eyes met. In Dorian's there was pity. He knew that what Alan was going to do was dreadful.

After a moment of silence he leaned across and said very quietly, but watching the effect of each word upon Alan's face.

---

in society, i.e. where the upper-class live and move
pale, without much colour

"Alan, in a locked room of this house a dead man is sitting at a table. He has been dead ten hours now. Don't look at me like that. Who the man is, why he died, how he died are matters that do not concern you. What you have to do is this..."

"Stop, Dorian. I don't want to know anything further. Whether what you told me is true or not true doesn't concern me. I refuse to be mixed up in your life. Keep your horrible secrets to yourself. They don't interest me any more."

"Alan, they will have to interest you. You are the man who is able to save me. I have no choice. Alan, you are a scientist. You know about chemistry and things like that. You have made experiments. What you have to do is to destroy the body that is upstairs. Nobody saw this person come into the house. Indeed, at the present moment he is supposed to be in Paris. He will not be missed for months. When he is missed, no trace of him must be found here. You, Alan, you must change him and everything that belongs to him into a handful of ashes that I may scatter in the air."

"You are mad, Dorian. Mad to imagine that I would raise a finger to help you. I will have nothing to do with this matter. Do you think I am going to risk my reputation for you? I don't want to know about your devil's work."

"It was a suicide, Alan."

"I am glad to hear that. But who drove him to it? You, I am sure."

"Do you still refuse to do this for me?"

"Of course, I refuse. I will have absolutely nothing to do with it. I should not be sorry to see you publicly *disgraced.* Nothing will make me make a step to help you. Ask some of your friends. Don't ask me."

"Alan, it was murder. I killed him. You don't know how he had made me suffer."

"Murder! Good Heavens, Dorian, is that what you have come down to? I shall not inform upon you. It is not my business. But I will have nothing to do with it."

"You must have something to do with it. If you don't help me I am ruined. They will hang me. Alan! Don't you understand? They will hang me for what I have done."

"There is no use *prolonging* this scene. I absolutely refuse to do anything in this matter. It is mad of you to ask me."

"You refuse?"

"Yes."

The same look of pity came into Dorian Gray's eyes. Then he took a piece of paper out of his pocket and handed it to Campbell.

Alan looked at him in surprise and then took up the paper and opened it. As he read it, his face became deadly pale and he fell back in his chair. After two or three minutes of terrible silence Dorian came up to him and put his hand upon his shoulder.

---

disgraced, having lost one's reputation or good name
prolong, to make longer

"I am so sorry for you, Alan," he murmured, "but you leave me no alternative. I had written this letter before you came. You see the address. If you don't help me, I will send it. You know what the result will be. You are going to help me. Now it is for me to dictate the *terms*."

Campbell buried his face in his hands and a shudder passed through him. He felt as if an iron ring was being slowly tightened round his forehead. The hand upon his shoulder weighed like a hand of *lead*. It seemed to crush him.

"I cannot do it," he said mechanically as if words could change things.

"You must. You have no choice."

He hesitated a moment.

"Is there a fire in the room upstairs?"

"Yes, there is a gas-fire."

"I shall have to go home and get some things from the laboratory."

"No, Alan, you must not leave the house. Write out on a sheet of paper what you want, and my servant will take a cab and bring the things back to you."

Campbell wrote a few lines and addressed the letter to his assistant. Dorian took the note and read it carefully. Then he rang the bell and gave it to his servant with orders to return as soon as possible and to bring the things with him.

As the hall door shut, Campbell got up from the chair and went over to the window. He was

---

terms, conditions
lead, very heavy metal

trembling all over. For nearly twenty minutes neither of the men spoke. The ticking of the clock was like the beat of a hammer.

When the clock struck one, Campbell turned round and looking at Dorian Gray saw that his eyes were full of tears. There was something in the purity of that beautiful sad face that made him *furious.*

"You are horrible, absolutely horrible!" he muttered.

"Hush, Alan, you have saved my life," said Dorian.

"Your life? Good heavens! What a life that is! You have gone from corruption to corruption, and now you have *culminated* in crime. In doing what I am going to do, what you force me to do, it is not your life that I am thinking of."

"Ah, Alan," murmured Dorian with a sigh, "I wish you had a thousandth part of the pity for me that I have for you." He turned away as he spoke and stood looking out at the garden. Campbell made no answer.

After about ten minutes the servant re-entered carrying a large *box of chemicals* with a long *coil of steel and platinum wire* and two rather

box of chemicals

coil of steel
and platinum wire

---

furious, very angry
culminate, to end up

curiously shaped iron clamps.

"Shall I leave the things here, sir?" he asked.

"Yes," said Dorian. "Leave them here. You can have the day to yourself, Francis. I am not dining at home, so I shall not need you."

"Thank you, sir," said the man, leaving the room.

"Now, Alan, there is not a moment to be lost. How heavy this box is! I'll take it for you. You bring the other things."

They left the room together.

When they reached the top landing, Dorian took out the key and turned it in the lock. Then he stopped. A shudder ran through him. He half opened the door. As he did so he saw the face of his portrait grinning in the sunlight. He remembered that the night before he had forgotten for the first time to hide the fatal canvas. He stepped back with a shudder.

What was that terrible red spot on one of the hands, as though the canvas was wet with blood? How horrible it was! — more horrible, it seemed to him, than the silent figure that was sitting in the room leaning on the table. Its grotesque shadow on the spotted carpet showed him that it was still there as he had left it. He stopped, afraid to turn round, with his eyes fixed on the picture. He heard Campbell bringing in the heavy box and the other things he needed for his dreadful work. He wondered if he and Basil Hallward had ever met and if so what they had thought of each other.

"Leave me now," said a stern voice behind him.

He turned and hurried out, leaving Campbell gazing into a yellow dead face. As Dorian was going downstairs, he heard the key being turned in the lock.

It was long after seven when Campbell came back into the library. He was pale but absolutely calm.

"I have done what you asked me to do," he muttered. "And now goodbye."

"You have saved my life, Alan. I will never forget it," said Dorian simply.

As soon as Campbell had left, he went upstairs. There was a horrible smell of nitric acid in the room. But the dead man sitting at the table had disappeared.

Chapter 11

A cold rain began to fall as Dorian Gray hurried along the street, repeating to himself the words that Lord Henry had said to him on the first day they met: "Cure the soul by means of the senses." How the words rang in his ears! His soul was certainly sick to death. Was it true that the senses could cure it? Innocent blood had been spilt. What could *atone* for that? For that there was no atonement. But though forgiveness was impossible, it was possible to forget, and he was determined to

---

atone, make repayment (e.g. for a crime)

forget, to *erase* everything from his memory, to kill the past. Indeed, what right had Basil to speak to him like that? Who had made him a judge over others? He had said things that were so dreadful and horrible that he could not bear them.

He bit his lip and for a few seconds his eyes grew sad. But only for a few seconds. He did not want to think of that. Each man lived his own life and paid his own price for living it. It was only a pity that one had to pay over and over again.

He hastened on quickening his step, but as he turned into a dim passage, that led to the ill-famed den where he was going, he felt somebody *seize* him from behind, and before he had time to defend himself, he was pushed back against the wall and a strong hand took him by the throat. He struggled madly for life and by a terrible effort tore the tightening fingers away. In a second he saw a revolver pointing straight at his head and a short *thick-set* man facing him.

"What do you want?" he gasped.

"Don't move," said the man. "If you move I will shoot you."

"You are mad. What have I done to you?"

"You ruined the life of Sibyl Vane," was the answer. "And Sibyl Vane was my sister. She killed herself, I know it. It is your fault and I swore I would kill you. For many years I have looked

---

erase, delete, wipe out
seize, take firm hold of
thick-set, having a broad, strong body

for you. I had no trace, no clue. The two people who could describe you — my mother and my sister — were dead. I knew nothing of you but the pet name she used to call you. Tonight I heard a woman in a pub call you 'Prince Charming'. Pray to God, for tonight you are going to die."

Dorian Gray grew sick with fear.

"I never knew her," he muttered. "I never heard of her. You are mad."

"You had better confess your sins, for as sure as I am James Vane, you are going to die." There was a horrible moment. "Down on your knees!" growled the man. "I give you one minute — no more. I am sailing for India tonight and I must do my job first. One minute. That's all."

Paralyzed with terror, Dorian did not know what to do. Suddenly a wild hope flashed across his brain.

"Stop," he cried. "How long ago did your sister die? Quickly, tell me!"

"Eighteen years," said the man. "Why do you ask me? What do years matter?"

"Eighteen years," laughed Dorian Gray with a touch of triumph in his voice. "Eighteen years! Put me under the lamp and look at my face!"

James Vane hesitated for a moment not understanding what he meant. Then he seized Dorian Gray and dragged him with him. Even in the dim light he could see his hideous mistake, for the face of the man he was going to kill had all the beauty of boyhood, all the purity of youth. He seemed no older than his sister had been when she died. It was clear that this was not the man who had destroyed her life. He let his hand go and stepped back.

"My God! my God!" he cried, "and I wanted to murder you!"

Dorian Gray drew a long breath.

"You were going to commit a terrible crime, my man," he said looking at him sternly. "Let this be a warning to you not to take *vengeance* into your own hands."

"Forgive me, sir," muttered James Vane. "I was mistaken. A chance word I heard in that pub."

As Dorian walked away, James Vane remained on the pavement. He was trembling. After a little while a black shadow that had been creeping along the wall moved out into the light and came close to him. He felt a hand on his shoulder and looked round with a start. It was one of the women he had seen in the pub.

"Why didn't you kill him?" she hissed, putting her drunken face close to his. "You fool! You should have killed him. He has lots of money and he is a real devil."

"He is not the man I am looking for," he answered, "and I don't want a man's money. I want a man's life. The man whose life I want must be nearly forty now. This one is a little more than a boy. Thank God I have not got his blood on my hands."

The woman gave a bitter laugh.

---

vengeance, punishment given in return (i.e. an eye for an eye)

"Little more than a boy! If you want to know, it is nearly eighteen years since Prince Charming made me what I am."

"You lie!" cried James Vane.

She raised her hands up to the Heaven.

"Before God I am telling the truth," she cried out. "He is the worst man that comes here. They say he has sold himself to the devil for a pretty face. It's nearly eighteen years since I met him. He hasn't changed much since then. Not like me," she added with a sad grin.

"You swear this?"

"I swear it!"

James Vane rushed to the corner of the street but Dorian Gray had disappeared. When he looked back the woman had gone too.

Chapter 12

The next day Dorian did not leave the house and spent most of the time in his room, sick with a terror of dying. When he closed his eyes he saw again and again the pale face of James Vane pressed against the window of the sitting-room watching him, and horror laid its hand upon his heart.

Perhaps it was only his fantasy. If any footmarks had been found on the flower beds, the gardeners would have informed him. Yes, it had been merely a fantasy. Sibyl Vane's brother had not come back to kill him. The mask of youth had saved him.

And yet, if it had been merely an illusion, how terrible it was to think that his guilty conscience could raise such fearful phantoms and make them move before him. As the thought crept through his brain he grew pale with terror, and the air seemed to him suddenly colder.

It was only on the third day that he decided to go out. After breakfast he walked for an hour in the garden and then drove across the park to join the party of hunters, including Lord Henry. At the corner of the *pine-wood* he saw Sir Geoffrey Clouston putting his gun to his shoulder. Dorian looked in the direction of the gun and saw a hare. As the hare reached the thicket, Sir Geoffrey fired. There were two cries heard: the cry of the wounded hare which was dreadful and the cry of a dying man which was even more dreadful.

"Good Heavens! I have hit a *beater*!" exclaimed Sir Geoffrey. "What an ass the man was to get in front of the guns."

Dorian watched him and the *head-keeper* move between the trees and in a few moments they appeared dragging a body after them. He turned away in horror. He heard Sir Geoffrey say that the man was really dead.

After a few moments that seemed to him like hours felt a hand on his shoulder.

---

pine-wood, wood of pine trees (fir trees)
beater, person who drives wild birds or animals towards the gun-shooters
head-keeper, person who looks after the wild animals on an estate

"Dorian," said Lord Henry. "I had better tell them to stop the shooting for today. It is not good to go on."

"Is the man..." He could not finish the sentence.

"I am afraid so," answered Lord Henry. "But it was his own fault. Why did he get in front of the guns? But there is no use talking about the matter."

Dorian shook his head.

"It is a bad *omen*, Henry. I feel as if something horrible is going to happen to some of us. To myself, perhaps," he added passing his hand over his eyes.

"What nonsense! There is no such thing as an omen. Besides what can happen to you, Dorian? You have everything in the world that a man can want. There is no one who would not be delighted to change places with you."

"There is no one with whom I would not change places, Henry. I have no terror of death. It is the coming of death that terrifies me."

"How absurdly nervous you are, my dear fellow. You must come and see my doctor when we get back to town."

* * *

At five o'clock Dorian Gray rang the bell for his servant and gave him orders to pack the things for the night-train to town. Then he wrote a note

---

omen, sign (often bad)

to Lord Henry telling him that he was going up to town to consult his doctor. As he was putting it into the envelope his servant came in and informed him that the head-keeper wished to see him.

"Send him in," he muttered after some moments' hesitation. As soon as the man entered, Dorian pulled his cheque-book and put it before him.

"I suppose you have come about the accident this morning, Thornton?" he said taking up a pen.

"Yes, sir," answered the keeper.

"Was the poor fellow married?" asked Dorian looking bored. "If so, I will send his family any sum of money you think necessary."

"We don't know who he is, sir. I never saw him before. Seems like a sailor, sir."

The pen dropped from Dorian Gray's hand and he felt as if his heart suddenly stopped beating.

"A sailor?" he cried out. "Did you say 'a sailor'?"

"Yes, sir. He looks as if he had been a sort of sailor: tattooed on both arms and that kind of thing."

Dorian leapt to his feet. A mad hope filled his heart.

"Where is the body?" he cried out. "Quick! I must see it at once."

"It is in an empty stable in the Home Farm, sir."

"The Home Farm! I'll go there at once."

In less than a quarter of an hour Dorian Gray was galloping down the road as fast as he could go. At last he reached the Home Farm. He leapt from the saddle and rushed to the farthest stable in which a light was seen. Something told him that the body was there.

At the door he paused for a moment feeling that he was going to make a discovery that would either bring him peace or ruin his life forever. Then he pushed the door and entered.

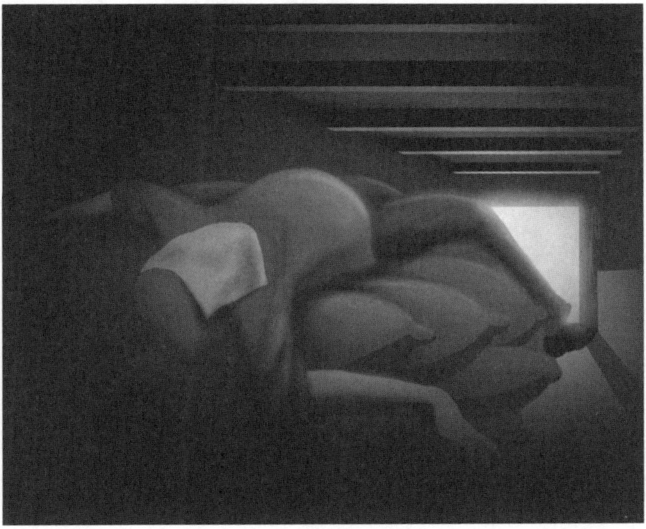

On a heap of sacks in the far corner lay the dead body of a man dressed in a coarse shirt and a pair of blue trousers. A spotted handkerchief had been placed on the face.

Dorian Gray shuddered. He felt that his hand could not take the handkerchief away and called out one of the farm servants to come to him.

"Take that thing off the face. I wish to see it." he said *clutching* at the door-post for support.

When the man had done so, he stepped forward. A cry of joy broke from his lips. The man who had been shot in the forest was James Vane. He stood there for some minutes looking at the dead body. As he rode home his eyes were full of tears, for he knew he was safe.

Chapter 13

"It is no use you telling me that you are going to be good," said Lord Henry. "You are already quite perfect. Please, don't change."

Dorian Gray shook his head.

"No, Harry, I have done too many dreadful things in my life. I am not going to do any more now. I began my good actions yesterday."

"And what was your good action?" asked his companion putting on his plate a little red pyramid of strawberries with white sugar upon them.

"I can tell you, Harry. It is not a story I could tell to anyone else. I spared a girl. She was very beautiful like Sibyl Vane. You remember Sibyl, don't you? How long ago that seems! Well, Hetty did not belong to our own class, of course. She was a simple village girl. But I really loved her. All during this wonderful May I used to see her two or three times a week. Yesterday she met me in a little garden. The apple-blossoms were falling on

---

clutch, to hold fast to

her hair and she was laughing. We were to go away together this morning at dawn. Suddenly I decided to leave her as pure and beautiful as I had found her."

"I think that new feeling must have given you real pleasure," said Lord Henry. "But I can finish your *idyll* for you. You gave her good advice and broke her heart. That was the beginning of your reformation."

"Harry, you mustn't say these dreadful things. Hetty's heart is not broken. Of course she cried and all that. But she is not disgraced."

water lilies

"And how do you know that Hetty isn't floating at the present moment in some *pond* with lovely *water lilies* round her like *Ophelia*?"

"I can't bear this, Harry! You mock everything and then suggest the most serious tragedies. I am sorry I told you. I don't care what you say to me. I know I was acting correctly. Don't let us talk about it any more and don't try to persuade me

---

idyll, perfect time or story
pond, smallish area of water
Ophelia, see note above. In her madness Ophelia drowned herself.

that the first good action I have done in years, the first *self-sacrifice* I have ever known is really a sort of sin. I want to be better. I am going to be better. Tell me something about yourself. What is going on in town? I have not been to the club for many days."

"The people are still discussing poor Basil's disappearance."

"I thought they had got tired of that by now," said Dorian pouring himself out some wine.

"My dear boy, they have only been talking about it for six weeks, and it is difficult for the British public to change the topic more often than every three months. They have been very fortunate lately, however. They have had my own divorce case and Alan Campbell's suicide. Now they have got the mysterious disappearance of an artist."

"What do you think has happened to Basil?" asked Dorian, surprised that he could discuss the matter so calmly.

"I have not the slightest idea. If Basil wants to hide himself, it is no business of mine. If he is dead, I don't want to think about him. Death is the only thing that terrifies me. I hate it."

"Why?"

"Because," said Lord Henry yawning, "one can survive everything nowadays except that."

"Harry, did it ever occur to you that Basil might have been murdered?"

---

self-sacrifice, giving up things you like in order to help others

Lord Henry raised his eyebrows in surprise.

"Why should he have been murdered? He was not clever enough to have enemies. Of course, he had a wonderful talent for painting but he was really rather dull. He only interested me once and that was when he told me years ago that he had a mad *adoration* for you and that you were the *dominant motive* of his art."

"I was very fond of Basil," said Dorian with a note of sadness in his voice. "But don't people say that he was murdered?"

"Oh, some of the papers do, but it does not seem to me probable. I know there are dreadful places in Paris, but Basil was not the sort of man to go to them. He had no curiosity. It was his chief *defect*."

"What would you say, Harry, if I told you that I had murdered Basil?" said Dorian.

"I would say that you were trying to play a part that doesn't suit you. Any crime is vulgar, just as any vulgarity is crime. And you, Dorian, cannot commit a crime. I am sorry if I hurt your *vanity* by saying so, but I am sure it is true. Besides, murder is always a mistake. One should never do anything that one cannot talk about after dinner. But let us stop talking about poor Basil. During the last ten years his painting had become much worse."

---

adoration, worship (see above)
dominant motive, main subject
defect, something missing or imperfect
vanity, favourable view of oneself

Dorian sighed.

"Yes," continued Lord Henry, "his painting had become much worse. When you and he stopped being friends, he stopped being a great artist. By the way, what has become of that wonderful portrait he did of you? I have never seen it, since he finished it. I remember you telling me years ago that you sent it to an exhibition and that it was stolen on the way. Hasn't it been found? What a pity! It was really a masterpiece. I remember I wanted to buy it."

Dorian went up to the piano and touched the keys.

"Play me something. Play me a *nocturne*, Dorian, and as you play, tell me in a low voice how you have kept your youth. You must have some secret. You have changed of course, but not in appearance. I wish you would tell me your secret. To get back my youth I would do anything in the world — except do morning exercises, or get up early or lead a *virtuous* life. Youth! There is nothing like it. The tragedy of old age is not that one is getting old but that in soul one remains young. Ah, Dorian, how happy you are! I wish I could change places with you. You are the type of man that our age is searching for."

Dorian rose from the piano and passed his hand through his hair.

---

nocturne, music-piece related to the night, especially soft piano music
virtuous, good (adjective from 'virtue')

"Yes, life has been wonderful," he murmured, "but I am not going to have the same life, Harry. You don't know everything about me. I think that if you did, even you would turn away from me."

"You and I will always be friends," said Lord Henry.

"And yet you poisoned me with a book once. I shall never forgive that. Harry, promise me that you will never give that book to anyone. It does harm."

"My dear boy, you are really beginning to *moralize*. You will soon be going about warning people against all the sins of which you have got tired! And I did not poison you by a book. Art has no influence upon a man's actions. It is quite neutral. The books that the world calls immoral are books that show the world its own vices. That is all. But we won't discuss literature. Come round tomorrow. I am going to ride at eleven. We might go together and I will take you to lunch afterwards with Lady Branksome. She is a charming woman and wants to consult you about some pictures she is going to buy."

"Must I really come, Harry?"

"Certainly. The *Park* is quite lovely now. I don't think there have been such lilacs since the year I met you."

---

moralize, speak about morals (and usually how they have fallen)

Park, i.e. Hyde Park in London

"Very well. I shall be here at eleven," said Dorian. "Good night, Harry."

As he reached the door he hesitated for a minute as if he had something more to say. Then he sighed and went out.

Chapter 14

It was a lovely night, so warm that he threw his coat over his arm and did not even put on his silk scarf. As he walked home smoking his cigarette, two young men in evening dress passed him. He heard one of them whisper to the other: "That is Dorian Gray". He remembered how pleased he used to be when he was pointed out or talked about. Now he was tired of hearing his own name. Half the charm of the little village where he had been so often lately was that no one knew who he was.

When he reached home he found his servant waiting for him. He sent him to bed, threw himself down on the sofa in the library and began to think over some of the things that Lord Henry had said to him.

The mirror, that Lord Henry had given to him so many years ago, was standing on the table and the *Cupids* laughed round it as before. He took it up, as he had done on that night of horror when he first noted the change in the fatal picture, and

---

Cupid, (Roman mythology) small god of love with wings and holding a bow and arrow

with wild eyes looked into it. It was his beauty that had ruined him, his beauty and the youth that he had prayed for. He threw the mirror on the floor and crushed it with his shoe. His beauty had been to him only a mask, his youth only a *mockery*. They had spoiled him.

It was better not to think of the past. It was of his future that he had to think. A new life! That was what he wanted. He had begun it already. He had spared an innocent girl. He would never do evil things again. He would be good.

As he thought of Hetty, he began to wonder if the portrait in the locked room had changed. He hoped it was not so horrible now as it had been. Perhaps if his life became pure, he would be able to remove every sign of evil passions from the face. Perhaps, the signs of evil had already gone away. He would go and look.

He took a lamp from the table and crept upstairs. He went in quietly, locking the door behind him as was his habit, and dragged the red coverlet from the portrait. A cry of pain and indignation broke from his lips. No change! Only in the eyes there was a new *cunning* look and in the mouth a hypocritical grin. The portrait was even more *loathsome*, if possible, than before, and the red spots on the hand seemed brighter and looked more like blood.

---

mockery, foolish and useless copy or example
cunning, clever at cheating
loathsome, extremely unpleasant

He trembled. Why was the red stain larger than it had been? There was blood on the painted feet as though it had dripped — and blood even on the hand that had not held the knife. Confess? Did it mean that he should confess? Give himself up and be put to death? He felt that the idea was monstrous. Besides, even if he did confess, who would believe him? There was no trace of the murdered man anywhere. Everything belonging to him had been destroyed. The world would simply say that he was mad. Yet, it was his duty to confess, to suffer public punishment and public shame. There was a God who called upon men to tell their sins to heaven and to earth. Should he really confess? Never. There was only one piece of evidence left against him — the portrait. He must destroy it. Why had he kept it so long? Once it had given him pleasure to watch it changing and growing old. But lately he had felt no such pleasure. It did not let him sleep at nights. It filled him with terror that other eyes could see his secret. It had poisoned for him many moments of joy. It was like a conscience to him. Yes, it was his conscience. He must destroy it. He looked round and saw the knife with which he had stabbed Basil Hallward. He had cleaned it many times till there was no stain of blood left on it. As it had killed the painter, so it would kill the painter's work and all that it meant. It would kill the past and when it was dead he would be free.

He seized the knife and stabbed the picture with it. There was a cry heard and something heavy fell on the floor. The cry was so horrible

that the frightened servants woke, rushed out of their rooms and crept upstairs. They knocked but there was no answer. They called out.

Everything was still. Finally, they got on up onto the roof and went down on the balcony. The windows opened easily. When they entered they found on the wall a lovely portrait of their master as they had last seen him in all his youth and beauty. Lying on the floor was a dead man in evening dress with a knife in his heart. He was ugly, wrinkled and loathsome. Only when they examined the rings on his hands did they recognize who it was.

Questions and Activities

Chapter 1

Questions

1. What atmosphere does Oscar Wilde create in the first paragraph?
2. Why did Lord Henry advise Basil to send the portrait to the Academy?
3. Why didn't Basil want to exhibit the portrait?
4. What is the only 'charm of marriage', according to Lord Henry?
5. What did Basil feel when he met Dorian Gray for the first time?
6. Did Dorian feel the same?
7. What did the painter ask Lord Henry not to do?
8. What signs are there in the chapter that we are in an upper-class milieu?

Activities

Say whether these statements are true or false. Correct them if they are false.

1) Lord Henry and Basil Hallward were old friends.

2) Lord Henry advised Basil to send the portrait to the Academy.
3) Basil wanted to exhibit the portrait of Dorian Gray.
4) It's better not to be different from others, according to Basil.
5) When Basil left London he never told anyone where he was going because he was hiding from the police.
6) Lord Henry was single.
7) In the picture of Dorian Gray Basil revealed his own soul.
8) When Basil Hallward saw Dorian for the first time he didn't pay attention to him.
9) Dorian and Basil felt at once that they were destined to know each other.
10) Basil didn't want Lord Henry to meet Dorian Gray because he was afraid that Dorian would spoil him.

Chapter 2

Questions

1. What impression did Dorian produce on Lord Henry?
2. Why didn't Basil want Lord Henry to stay?
3. Why did Dorian feel a pang of jealousy when he saw his portrait?
4. What wish did he express looking at the portrait?

5. Why did Basil Hallward want to destroy his work?
6. Why did Lord Henry's ideas confuse Dorian?
7. What is the main idea of new Hedonism? Discuss the morals of this attitude.
8. What did the painter do with the portrait?

Activities

1. Basil says, "Would you think it awfully rude if I asked you to leave?"
   Think of all the other ways that he could have said this.

2. Choose the right answer.

   A. Dorian wanted Basil ...

      1) to go away.
      2) to paint his full-size portrait.
      3) to give him the music of Schumann.

   B. Basil was afraid that Lord Henry ...

      1) would persuade Dorian not to sit for him.
      2) would have a bad influence on Dorian.
      3) would tell Dorian some facts from his (Basil's) life.

   C. Dorian Gray ...

      1) did not like Lord Henry at first.
      2) took a fancy to him from the first meeting.
      3) did not pay attention to his words.

D. Lord Henry thought that the only thing worth having is ...

   1) youth.
   2) money.
   3) a good reputation.

E. Dorian wanted ...

   1) to buy the portrait.
   2) to be always young.
   3) to deny pleasures.

F. Basil wanted to destroy the picture because

   1) he did not like it.
   2) he could not do what Dorian wanted.
   3) he did not want it to ruin their lives.

3. Take as many pages as you can from this chapter and dramatize them using three speakers. Perhaps you can imagine that this is a radio broadcast.

Chapter 3

Questions

1. How long had Dorian known Sibyl?
2 Where did Dorian meet Sibyl Vane for the first time?
3. How did she look?
4. Why did he fall in love with her?

5. How did Dorian Gray change from the boy Lord Henry had met in Basil's studio?
6. Dorian was sure that his friends would like Sibyl's acting, wasn't he?
7. How did Lord Henry explain Basil's habit to give good advice?
8. What did Dorian inform his friends about in the telegram?

Activities

1. Say why

   1) Lord Henry was late.
   2) people marry, according to Lord Henry.
   3) one evening Dorian decided to go out in search of some adventure.
   4) Dorian decided to go to the little theatre.
   5) Dorian was so impressed by the girl.
   6) Dorian wanted his friends to go and see Sibyl act.
   7) Dorian was jealous of the picture.
   8) Basil was a bore (from the point of view of Lord Henry).

2. In pairs, imagine Dorian and Lord Henry's dialogue about love updated to today.
   One of you has just fallen hopelessly in love, the other doesn't believe in love at all.
   Perhaps you could write a dialogue of 10 or 20 lines that you could act out for the class.

Chapter 4

Questions

1. Did Sibyl want to be rich?
2. What did her mother want her to do?
3. Why didn't Basil believe that Dorian wanted to marry a little actress?
4. What was Basil afraid of?
5. Why wasn't Lord Henry an advocate of marriage?
6. Where did Dorian go after the performance?
7. What was Lord Henry's theory about women?
8. How did Dorian describe his feelings?

Activities

1. Substitute the italicized words for their antonyms from the box — in their correct forms.

foolish
whisper
adore
private
wealth
contempt
handsome
poor
dreadful
gloomy

1) Dorian thought that Sibyl's acting was *wonderful*.
2) I think that his reply was very *clever*. And you?

3) She felt *respect* for her former husband.
4) *Poverty* may change a person's character.
5) When I saw this actor for the first time I was amazed to see how *ugly* he was.
6) I don't like this dress: it's too *bright*.
7) Basil Hallward *hated* Dorian Gray.
8) Sibyl lived in a *luxurious* flat.
9) "I'm so happy," *shouted* the girl.
10) Her son goes to a *public* school.

2. In pairs, imagine a dialogue of today that begins as follows:

   A: You won't believe this!
   B: Go on, tell me!
   A: X has got engaged to Y. (choose your own names)
   B: But I thought that...

Chapter 5

Questions

1. How did the audience react to Sibyl's acting?
2. Why did she seem to Dorian's friends absolutely untalented?
3. Why did she act so badly?
4. How did Dorian explain to Sibyl his disappointment in her?
5. Was Sibyl angry with Dorian for his words?
6. What change in the portrait did Dorian notice?
7. Did Dorian regret what he had done to the girl?
8. Why did he put a screen in front of the picture?

Activities

1. Match the nouns from the left column with the adjectives from the right column. All the answers are in the chapter.

flower	immense
voice	complete
heat	rude
gesture	artificial
manners	mad
failure	dim
animal	terrible
joy	faded
wish	wounded
light	shrill

2. In pairs, imagine a dialogue of today that begins as follows:

   A: I'm sorry, but it's all over between us.
   B: Why, what have I done wrong?
   A: You have disappointed me. I thought that you were different, something special, but now I see that you're just like all the rest.
   B: How dare you! Who do you think you are? It's *you* who are the disappointment!

Chapter 6

Questions

1. Why did Dorian start when his eyes fell on the screen?
2. Did the portrait alter?

3. What did the portrait make Dorian realize?
4. What did he write in his letter to Sibyl?
5. Dorian was shocked to hear about Sibyl's death, wasn't he?
6. Was Dorian afraid of the inquiry?
7. How did Dorian's feelings change after his conversation with Lord Henry?
8. Why does Dorian go to the opera in spite of Sibyl's death?

Activities

1. Say whether these statements are true or false. Correct them if they are false.

1) The picture made Dorian realize how cruel he had been to Sibyl.
2) He decided to destroy the portrait.
3) Dorian learned about Sibyl's death from newspapers.
4) Dorian didn't want Lord Henry to see the portrait.
5) Dorian wasn't afraid of the inquiry.
6) Sibyl's death was due to an accident.
7) Lord Henry was shocked by Dorian's words.
8) Dorian refused to go to the opera with Lord Henry.

2. In groups of three imagine that you are reporters and photographers for a modern newspaper/magazine covering the story of Sibyl Vane. Make up full front-page with three separate articles and six photographs. If you have a camera, you can actually take the photos!

Chapter 7

Questions

1. What was Basil afraid of when he learned the news about Sibyl's death?
2. What did Dorian really do?
3. Whom did Basil blame for the change in Dorian?
4. How did Dorian explain the girl's death to Basil?
5. Where did Dorian hide the portrait?
6. What was the result of the inquiry of Sibyl Vane's death?
7. Why was Dorian angry with Lord Henry?
8. What was the book that Lord Henry gave Dorian about?

Activities

1. Choose the right answer.

A. Basil learned about Sibyl's death ...

1) from Dorian.
2) from Lord Henry.
3) from a newspaper.

B. Dorian did not want to listen about Sibyl because ...

1) he felt it was his fault.
2) he was no longer interested in her.
3) he was in love with Harry's sister.

C. Dorian refused to sit to Basil again because ...

1) he was tired of sitting.
2) Lord Henry told him not to do it.
3) he thought there was something fatal about his portraits.

D. Dorian did not want Basil to look at the portrait because ...

1) he was afraid that Basil would see the change in his face.
2) he was afraid that Basil would take away the portrait.
3) he was afraid that Basil would destroy it.

E. He hid the portrait ...

1) in the library.
2) in a room upstairs.
3) in the hall.

F. A verdict on Sibyl's case was ...

1) a murder.
2) an accident.
3) a suicide.

G. Dorian ...

1) hated the book Harry had sent him.
2) was fascinated by it.
3) was not interested in it.

2. Imagine that the picture of Dorian Gray could speak to him. Make up a dialogue beginning as follows:

Picture: Hallo, Dorian. Do you recognize me?
Dorian: No, I've never seen you before!
Picture: Don't lie to me, Dorian. I don't like liars.
Dorian: I'm not lying!!!
Picture: Why did you hide me, Dorian?

Chapter 8

Questions

1. Why did Dorian like the book Lord Henry gave him?
2. Why didn't people believe the evil rumours about Dorian?
3. How did Dorian react to the contrast between the face on the canvas and the face that he saw in the glass?
4. Why did Dorian make no sign of recognition when he met Basil Hallward?
5. Where was Basil going?
6 What did Basil want to speak to Dorian about?
7. Dorian made the name of Harry's sister a by-word, didn't he?
8. Why did Dorian decide to show the portrait to Basil?

Activities

1. Say which word in each line do not fit with the other.
   1) artist, scientist, martyr, judge
   2) mirror, canvas, armchair, sofa
   3) delightful, remarkable, indecent, extra-ordinary
   4) travel, handbag, luggage, suitcase
   5) fog, mist, rain, cold
   6) shameful, decent, vicious, ill-famed
   7) kind, fair, pure, evil
   8) back, tongue, lips, mouth

2. Say whether these statements are true or false. Correct them if they are false.
   1) Unlike the novel's hero Dorian never lost his beauty.
   2) Dorian did not recognize Basil Hallward when he met him.
   3) Basil believed the rumours about Dorian.
   4) Hypocrites are people who follow the principles of New Hedonism.
   5) People said that Dorian corrupted everyone with whom he became friends.
   6) Basil did not believe that he could see Dorian's soul.
   7) Dorian decided to show the portrait to the painter because he wanted to share his secret with him.
   8) Dorian thought that Basil was to blame for his corruption.

3. Dorian says, "You forget that we live in the land *of hypocrites.*"
   Look around you in your own local or national environment and find examples of hypocrites — including perhaps yourself!

Chapter 9

Questions

1. What did the room look like?
2. Did Basil recognize Dorian's face in the picture?
3. What did Dorian remind Basil of?
4. How did Basil react to Dorian's words?
5. Why did Dorian stab Basil Hallward?
6. What did Dorian do after he had killed Basil?
7. Why wasn't Dorian afraid that Basil's disappearance would be discovered?
8. Why did he ask his servant about the time?

Activities

1. Put these sentences in the right order, according to the text.

   1) A feeling of hatred for Basil Hallward came over Dorian.
   2) Dorian tore the curtain from the portrait.
   3) Basil realized that it was the portrait he had made.
   4) Dorian and Basil went upstairs.
   5) Dorian took out the key and turned it in the lock.

6) Dorian went out of the house and began ringing the bell.
7) Basil seized the lighted candle and held it to the picture.
8) Dorian dug the knife into Hallward.
9) Dorian began to look for the address of Alan Campbell.
10) Dorian put Basil's bag and coat in a secret wall-cabinet.

2. Draw a cartoon series of six pictures with speech bubbles to illustrate the events of this chapter.

Chapter 10

Questions

1. How did Dorian look when his servant came into his room?
2. Why was he horribly nervous waiting for the reply to his letter to Alan Campbell?
3. What precisely did Dorian want Alan to do?
4. Why did Alan Campbell first refuse to obey Dorian?
5. But why did he then agree?
6. What did Alan say about Dorian's life?
7. What was on one of the hands of the figure on the canvas?
8. How, do you think, did Campbell destroy the dead man?

Activities

1. Say why...
    1) Dorian killed Basil Hallward.
    2) Dorian wanted to see Alan Campbell.
    3) every face that Dorian drew had a fantastic likeness to Basil Hallward.
    4) Dorian was so nervous while waiting for Alan.
    5) Alan didn't want to help Dorian.
    6) Alan finally agreed to do what Dorian wanted him to.
    7) Dorian was sure that Basil would not be missed for months.
    8) Dorian didn't let Alan leave the house.
    9) Dorian shuddered when he saw the portrait.
    10) there was a smell of nitric acid in the room.

2. Imagine that Alan Campbell goes directly from Dorian to the police in a state of shock. Make up his conversation with the policeman beginning as follows:

    Alan: There's been a murder!
    Policeman: Yes sir, and who is the victim?
    Alan: Basil Hallward.
    Policeman: And where is the body?
    Alan: Er, I, er...

Chapter 11

Questions

1. What was Dorian determined to do?
2. How did Dorian try to justify himself? (to free himself from blame?)
3. What happened when he turned in to a dim passage?
4. Why did the man want to kill Dorian?
5. What did the man know about Dorian?
6. Why didn't he kill Dorian?
7. What did the woman tell James Vane?
8. Do you admire Dorian for being smart?

Activities

1. Say which of the words is the odd one.

   1) shoot, murder, kill, defend
   2) vicious, spoiled, innocent, monstrous
   3) cure, treat, heal, survive
   4) smell, sight, hearing, breathing
   5) seize, move, rush, creep
   6) ruin, destroy, create, destruct
   7) bargain, sell, buy, swear
   8) apartment, flat, den, lodging

2. Complete the sentences using the book.

   1) Dorian's soul was ...
   2) Dorian was determined ...
   3) Each man pays ...

4) As Dorian turned into a dim passage he felt ...
5) In a second he saw a revolver ...
6) For many years the man ...
7) Sibyl's brother didn't kill Dorian Gray because ...
8) The woman from the pub told James Vane that ...
9) People said that Dorian ...
10) James Vane rushed after Dorian Gray but ...

3. Imagine that you are James Vane. Tell your friends about your sister and your meeting Dorian Gray near a pub.

Chapter 12

Questions

1. Why did Dorian stay in his room for two days?
2 Why did he feel remorse?
3. What were the people doing in the pine-wood when he joined them?
4. Why didn't Dorian want to kill a hare?
5. Was the shot man a beater?
6. What did Dorian feel when he heard that a man had been shot?
7. Why did Dorian's heart stop beating when he learnt that the dead man looked like a sailor?
8. Did Dorian cry for joy or for pity?

Activities

1. Match the nouns from the left column with the adjectives from the right column.

1. man	1. bad
2. phantoms	2. dreadful
3. fingers	3. dying
4. hours	4. leaden
5. wings	5. dead
6. air	6. monstrous
7. hope	7. endless
8. body	8. icy
9. image	9. fearful
10. omen	10. mad

2. Say whether these statements are true or false. Correct them if they are false.

1) Dorian did not leave the house because he was ill.
2) He did not feel any remorse.
3) On the third day Dorian drove to the opera.
4) He told his companion not to kill a bear.
5) Sir Geoffrey thought that he had hit a beater.
6) Dorian at once understood that the dead man was Sibyl's brother.
7) He thought that this murder was a bad omen.
8) Dorian said that he would not like to change places with anyone.
9) He wanted to give money to the man's family.
10) In the stable he himself took the handkerchief away from the man's face.

3. The chapter begins with Dorian being "sick with the terror of dying" and ends with his eyes "full of tears, for he knew he was safe".

   Imagine at this point that Dorian visits either
   a) a priest, to whom he confesses, or
   b) a psychologist, to whom he tries to lie.

   Make up a conversation between Dorian and the priest or the psychologist.

Chapter 13

Questions

1. What was Dorian's good action?
2 What were the people discussing in the club?
3. Why didn't Harry want to think about Basil if he was dead?
4. Why didn't he believe that the painter had been murdered?
5. What did Dorian tell him about the portrait?
6. How did Lord Henry explain the tragedy of old age?
7. What did Dorian accuse his friend of?
8. Did Lord Henry agree that he had poisoned Dorian with the book?

Activities

Based on your own personal experience discuss Harry's statement: "Art has no influence upon a man's actions".

Chapter 14

Activities

1. Say why
   1) Dorian went to a small village.
   2) Dorian felt a longing for the purity of his boyhood.
   3) he began to hate his beauty.
   4) he spared an innocent girl.
   5) Dorian decided to look at the portrait.
   6) a cry of pain and indignation broke from his lips when he saw the portrait.
   7) he decided to destroy the portrait.
   8) the servants at first did not recognize him.

2. Imagine that you are one of Dorian's servants. Make up the conversation with a detective about what you saw upstairs, beginning as follows:

   You: There was blood everywhere!!!

   Policeman: Was there any sign of a break-in?

   You: I didn't look. No, that's impossible. There's no way out except through the door.

   Policeman: Did you have a key to the door?